Keith Waterhouse

In a long and successful career, Keith Waterhouse has published fourteen novels, including *Billy Liar*, seven collections of journalism, and seven non-fiction books, including two volumes of memoirs, *City Lights* and *Streets Ahead*. He has written widely for television, cinema and the theatre, including the long-running play *Jeffrey Bernard is Unwell*, and writes an award-winning column for the *Daily Mail*. Also published by Sceptre are his novels *There is a Happy Land*, *Our Song*, *Bimbo*, *Unsweet Charity*, *Good Grief*, and his most recent, *Soho*.

ALSO BY KEITH WATERHOUSE

KEITH WATERHOUSE

Palace Pier

Hodder and Stoughton
A division of Hodder Headline
338 Euston Road
London NW1 3BH

SCEPTRE

Copyright © 2003 Keith Waterhouse

First published in Great Britain in 2003 by Hodder and Stoughton
A division of Hodder Headline

A Sceptre Paperback

1 3 5 7 9 10 8 6 4 2

A CIP catalogue record for this title is
available from the British Library

ISBN 0 340 82301 1

Typeset in Sabon by Palimpsest Book Production Limited,
Polmont, Stirlingshire

Printed and bound in Great Britain by
Clays Ltd, St Ives plc

Palace Pier

FRIDAY

1

A creature of habits, this Chris Duffy. The Woolworth alarm clock is set for eight: he is up at eight. Unless it has been one of those nights, when it could be nine. Ten, when it seriously has been one of those nights. Never later than ten thirty, which is opening time down here in Brighton.

First things first. Routine. Shit-shave-shower, in double-quick order. Considering his lax, grazing-on-the-hoof eating pattern throughout the day, which goes against his otherwise strict regime, it is surprising how regular he manages to be. Duffy puts it down to the bran flakes.

After, or on occasion with, the bran flakes, the miniature Smirnoff vodka. Never more than one, and never bigger than a miniature. Would be cheaper to buy it a quarter-bottle at a time, half a bottle even, but you do not catch Duffy out that way. Discipline. What he calls the first of the few. A miniature. Neat. In lieu of coffee.

With his gulp of vodka, Duffy browses through his copy of the *Guardian*. Delivered each morning, although not to him personally but to his landlady Maureen upstairs, who takes it together with her *Daily Telegraph* and leaves it outside the door of what she chooses to call the garden flat, although there is no garden.

He scans the letters page. Nothing from Chris Duffy, Brighton; although he banged not a bad one off a couple of days ago. If (Leader, Wednesday) the volume of methane produced by cattle is sufficient to meet a substantial proportion of the world's energy needs, doesn't that leave the Department of the Environment, Food, Rural Affairs &c &c in the shit? Chris Duffy, Brighton.

Not one of his best, on reflection. He always aims these shots at what he calls the smart-arse corner, the first column of short, snappy letters from student-sounding types with names like Dave, Pete or Roz. Not sharp enough. Not smart-arse enough.

He has a better idea for today. In your corrections and clarifications column, you apologised for saying that the deputy chairman of the Press Complaints Commission is seventy, rather than seventy-one. Did he complain? And if so, why did he bother?

Possibly not. Few of Duffy's letters reach the getting-sent-off stage, and only a handful have ever been printed. Two, in fact. He keeps them, now tattered, in his wallet. The first was about an impending rail strike on the Brighton line which asked succinctly how anyone would know. The second, in response to an item about the National Theatre losing its royal title, asked why there were so many Theatre Royals in this country when to the best of his knowledge the royal family had never set foot in any of them.

These letters represent Duffy's entire published output over the past two years. There is a second novel on the way – a third, he should say, if you count his unpublished

4

one, *The Golden Mile* – but he is having writer's-block problems with that. Maybe he'll take a long walk along the seafront this morning and get it sorted.

No, not this morning, he was forgetting it is Friday, and Friday he always has to have the one first thing in the Swan with Two Necks with what he laughingly calls his staff. Eggo, as Edgar has always been known, after the old ostrich character in the *Beano* comic, on account of his unusually long neck. Standing arrangement. Bit of a village idiot, Eggo, but he has his uses.

Saturday mornings, he opens up the bric-à-brac stall Duffy operates in North Laines. Repro, Fifties, bit of sub-art deco when he can get his fists on it, all that's left of All Our Yesterdays, the shop he set up off Trafalgar Street with his ex-partner Jackie, or she set up with him, before she cleared off like the other one. These days he only deals with dealers, insofar as he deals with anybody. Buys the stuff from one set of mates, flogs it to another, puts the rest on the barrow, bangs on coded price tickets, leaves it to Eggo.

Duffy is to be found Saturday mornings in one of three pubs where Eggo can seek him out if there's anyone wanting to do a spot of bargaining. Give him a trade price, pay him his commission, knock it on the head at lunchtime, and that's it. The business is running gently into the ground but who gives a toss? Duffy wasn't brought upon this earth to sell sub-art deco. Duffy is a writer.

Tappety-tap on the inside door. Maureen.

'Are you up and decent?'

'No, I'm lying on the bed, stark bollock naked.'

5

'Chance would be a fine thing.'

This, or a variation of it, is a daily routine. She has put her head round the door. Now she is about to remind him he owes the rent.

'You know what date it is, don't you, Chris? Only.'

'I'll have it for you tomorrow afternoon, Maureen.'

'Let's hope so. Otherwise.'

Maureen, who must be Duffy's age by now although looking younger, has the air of a veteran pub landlady. Not far out: she did at one time work in the Whip Tavern in Trafalgar Street, which is where Duffy met her when it was his local. Husband died, left her a bit of money, now she stays at home and writes, or claims to, although Duffy has never caught her at it. Unlike him, never had anything published.

'So shall I see you about threeish, or?'

'If you're up for it, Maureen.'

'It's more whether you're up for it. Don't get too pissed.'

She chooses the area steps door rather than the inside one that leads upstairs. So she's going straight out, then. Her Friday shop. He watches her along Sheridan Square. Good legs, still. Waits a few minutes in case she has to come back for something, then pads upstairs and lets himself into her flat with the spare key she leaves under the stair carpet. She'll be about half an hour. Should fill in the time very nicely before they open.

Like his own bedsitter, Maureen's flat, two rooms and usual offices, has an Edwardian feel to it, having been furnished from North Laine junk shops. The flat above it, occupied by a street trader like himself, Mickey

6

Daniels, is the same. Should be out at this hour, flogging the same kind of gear that furnishes the little flintstone-clad terrace house, reputedly one of a set of former fishermen's cottages. Either that or prowling about the place like a cat, as is his wont, looking for some further unconsidered trifle to put out on his stall, a secret smile playing on his lips as if he is savouring a private joke. Duffy could prove that he is gradually selling off Maureen's bits and pieces. But it is none of his business.

Up and beyond Mickey Daniels, on the top floor, more of an attic really, lives Olive, seventy-odd, surname unknown to Duffy. No doubt her flat too is like something out of the 1910 Army & Navy Stores catalogue but Duffy wouldn't know, he has never set foot in it. Mickey, who has, says it is a tip. Olive is given to stashing away old newspapers, plastic shopping bags and bits of cardboard by the bale, not only her own but the contents of other people's rubbish sacks which she raids on a daily basis, the while chuntering to herself. Mickey says she ought to be sectioned. At least, reflects Duffy, she doesn't go around smirking to herself like a dyspeptic Cheshire cat.

So where was he, last time he was here in Maureen's flat without her present? The chest of drawers, nothing there, done that. The desk, first place he'd looked, if you can call it a desk. More a stripped-pine kitchen dresser with one drawer, supporting an old Olivetti manual typewriter and a jumble of typing paper and spiral notebooks. Drawer crammed with rejected short stories. Women's stuff, not bad, some of it, but not what he's looking for.

7

The wardrobe. Nothing of interest in the hanging cupboards and the long bottom drawer's locked, as always. But this time he's brought a key. Maureen's wardrobe is more or less a duplicate of his own, the kind of thing you could find in that old Army & Navy Stores catalogue or in those repro Heal's catalogues they sell along with the kids' annuals on the Days Gone By bookstall. Place where he once bought that batch of 1960s *Lilliput* mags with stories by Bill Naughton. Duffy could have written those, or similar. But the bastards would never use any of his stuff, bastardising bastards that they were.

With any luck his key should fit. It does. The deep wardrobe drawer is stiff, hasn't been opened for an age, needs a drop of oil. Holy Christ, it's like a licensed sex shop in there. Rubber, leather, fishnet, fur-lined handcuffs – stuff you'd find in the window of the Boutique Bleu off North Street, which is probably where it all came from. Duffy has never set eyes on any of this gear before, even though he's well aware that Maureen does have a kinky streak. It just goes to strengthen the suspicion he's always had about Maureen: that at some point in her chequered career she has been on the game.

Nothing to do with Duffy. He closes the drawer with difficulty, locks it, and, ears pricked, listens.

Creaking stairs. Not coming up, so it can't be Maureen back already, and anyway she'd use the front door and he would have heard her opening it. No, going down. Olive? Bit early for her. Like everyone else in the house – everyone in Brighton, if you ask Duffy – she likes her drop, but not usually this side of noon.

No, the footfall's too heavy for Olive. It's got to be Mickey Daniels, lazy sod that he is, why isn't he out grafting?

That's his comical om-tiddly-om-pom knock. Is he giving Maureen one? No, surely not, she's too old for him, and he's still of an age where he can pull all he needs in the clubs. So what's the crafty sod up to? He knocks again, rattles the doorknob, retreats. Now he must be feeling under the staircase for Maureen's latchkey. But Duffy has that. It's getting to be like that Hitchcock film, *Dial M for Murder*. Mickey comes back to the door, knocks again, shakes the doorknob.

'Hello – who's in there?'

Nothing for it. Duffy has to open the door.

'Thought you were at work,' Duffy says.

Smiling like Peter Lorre, Mickey steps swiftly over the threshold. 'Yes, I can see you did. What you on, then, Duffy?'

'Who's to say I'm on anything?'

Mickey's quick eyes, like optic anteaters, dart about the room. Nothing. But he's not satisfied. No reason why he should be. The half-smile fluttering on his lips, he cheekily opens Maureen's bedroom door and takes a comprehensive look around, like a policeman. Nothing.

'Put it this way, what are you doing in Maureen's flat?'

'Come to that, Mickey, what are you doing in it?'

'You let me in.'

'You would have let yourself in if you'd found the key. What do you want?'

'I asked first.'

Mickey's eyes resume their roving quest. So he's not necessarily trying to incriminate Duffy, he's looking for something. As a street trader, Mickey is gifted with serendipity. He finds what he wants – a fussy-looking, deep-red enamelled vase with gold oriental embossments, Japanese at a guess. It's standing in the fireplace, half concealed behind an Edwardian curtained screen, and filled with dried flowers. A still life of domestic neglect. Mickey picks the vase up, careful to leave the dead blooms intact. They would be evidence, otherwise.

'Tell you what, Duffy. I haven't seen you and you haven't seen me, fair enough?'

Duffy doesn't do old vases if he can help it. The punters tend to drop them on the pavement while knowledgeably checking for cracks. Besides, it could be fairground tat for all he knows. Or cares. Duffy has never been all that knowledgeable about what he has always regarded as the second string to his bow. He used to leave the expertise to Jackie. He has since bought a big thick paperback manual of antique prices with copious illustrations like that 1910 Army & Navy Stores catalogue, but he is yet to get very far with it.

'What do you want it for? It looks like junk to me.'

'On its own, it's not worth a light. But as a pair . . .'

'And you've got the other one, is that it?'

Or rather, Maureen had the other one, and Mickey has at some point acquired it. No concern of Duffy's.

At the door, clutching his purloined vase, Mickey smiles: 'So you're not about to tell me what you're on?'

'Not nicking Maureen's gear, that's for sure.'

'Don't worry, Duffy, I'll get it out of you. You in the Crown and Two later?'

'Might be, might not be.'

It makes no difference whether he gets into the Crown and Two Chairmen or not. Mickey Daniels will catch up with him, cling to him, like the seaweed washing up on the shore.

2

Still twelve and a half minutes to opening-time. Duffy saunters around Sheridan Square and takes the sloping street down to the seafront, just west of the Palace Pier. Brighton Pier as they choose to call it now, with its name spelled out in electric light bulbs, to put two fingers up to the still-derelict West Pier along the beach. But to Brighton's floating population, it will forever be the Palace Pier.

There's activity, of a sort. Bit early for this kind of thing. Two or three stilt-walkers with Clown Joey faces, working the esplanade and hassling the punters with inane lipstick grins and squeakers. A fire-eater and two samba drummers setting out their gear. A Pygmalion statue act, where a girl painted blue from head to toe like a turquoise Madonna stands on a beer crate, shivering in the cold morning sunlight.

Must be something going on. Duffy, who cannot abide street theatre, shuffles along the front, eyes averted. He would cross over the road to the Doctor Brighton's pub but it's still too early. As for the Swan with Two Necks and dozy Eggo, when did that ever open before ten forty-five earliest, lazy sods that they are? He has decided to walk along the esplanade as far as the Jackdaw in Waterloo Street bordering Hove – Hove Actually, as

13

it's still known to locals for all that the two towns, Brighton and Hove, are now Siamese-twinned as one city, while a move to pair them New York-style as BriHo has spectacularly fallen on its face – and have the first one there.

A top-hatted Edwardian-looking figure in a bottle-green tailcoat is now pedalling a penny-farthing along the front to join the stilt-walkers and the fire-eater, the tip of a forty-foot-or-so chimney-sweep's rod balanced on his shoulder, the other end supported by a unicyclist fetching up the rear and juggling with two dinner plates. A pole-squatting act, then. Whatever is beginning to happen, it is warming up.

It's a breezy late spring or early summer day, good for blowing away hangovers, if he had one. Which he never does, these days, apart from the tiredness. Worries him sometimes: how can you live Duffy's kind of life and not feel the effects of it? They could be piling up, to get him when least expected.

One effect that does get through is that the old memory's going. Backing momentarily against the wind gusting up from the west, he can just make out through the sea haze a banner flapping across the Palace Pier. Brighton Festival. Hence the street theatre. Kick-off today – he'd totally forgotten about it. Photo-call at noon for whoever's arrived by that time, then open house – well, cash bar for the likes of Duffy, to be brutally frank – in the foyer of the Brighton Dome.

Duffy will be there. Duffy likes a festival, within reason, especially the literary end. Some of them, anyway. He remembers years and years ago now, when he was still living in Blackpool, crossing the Pennines to the Ilkley Festival. Sat up till dawn chatting up Anthony Burgess, drinking their own weight in brandy. How they demolished poor John Braine, at that time flavour of the month. 'A one-book man,' said Burgess. 'And he's yet to write it.' What a night that was.

But there were some of these festivals, you were made to feel as if you'd come to the door selling chamois leathers. Snooty, they were, just because you hadn't had a book out this particular year and didn't have an invite.

Brighton will be OK. Brighton knows him. He'll be there.

He strides on along the esplanade, kicking the pebbles thrown up by last night's high winds. Few people on the beach. A lighter on the horizon, headed for Shoreham. No pleasure boats in sight. It is how Duffy prefers it. He likes to think of Brighton as a seafaring town, despite all the evidence, rather than a seaside resort. Perhaps he is hankering after his native Fleetwood.

Salt in his blood, Duffy likes to boast when given half a chance, to create the impression that he's a bit of an old sea dog. To a limited extent it is true: he has never lived anywhere that wasn't a pebble's throw from a beach.

So: born in Blackpool, or to be more precise Fleetwood, 11 Jan. 1940, as it would say in *Who's Who* if he were in it. Father a corporation transport supervisor, downgraded in Duffy's CV to a tram driver. Grammar school. Narrowly escaped National Service call-up. Became Town Hall clerk, got into writing inspired by

Gerald Kersh short stories, had germ of idea for novel based on local government life but beaten to it by John Braine, the bastard.

Fall-out with father over heavy lunchtime drinking at Yates's Wine Lodge and getting in with bad crowd of fairground types. Moves into digs behind Winter Gardens: various casual jobs, mainly on the Pleasure Beach, otherwise the Golden Mile – working on the helter-skelter, rifle range, roller-coaster, scenic railway, big dipper, Noah's Ark, and as a barker, barman and waffle-tosser.

Out of all this he gets a novel, bashed out on a second-hand portable Corona, which is published as *Razzle-Dazzle*, a *roman-à-clef* or slice of life. So ripe a slice, indeed, that several of his friends boast of being in it, while one, a deck-chair attendant named Eric Alladyce, claims to have more or less dictated most of the novel to Duffy in Yates's Wine Lodge.

Beyond the South Shore, however, and outside the pages of the *Blackpool Gazette* and the odd 'In brief' paragraph in the literary columns, *Razzle-Dazzle* created little stir. A second novel, *The Golden Mile*, was turned down as being too like the first.

But that was then and this is now, although it is one of the days when he wishes now was then. At the approach of another street-theatre tableau, in the shape of two human marionettes got up as Groucho and Harpo in control of one another's strings, Duffy lurches smartly across the road to the forecourt of the Metropole Hotel. To the accompaniment of celestial strings coaxed out of the spokes of a bicycle wheel by Harpo, a stretch limo draws up and the chauffeur leaps out to open one of its many doors.

It is fortunate that Duffy is wearing his writing gear, rather than, say, the standard Brighton cheque-bouncing set of blazer and cravat. He is every inch the scribbler in black polo-neck sweater, medallion, bleached jeans, trainers, bomber jacket. As a familiar figure steps out of the limo he completes the image by donning the dark glasses he always carries, and pushing them up over his receding hairline.

A familiar figure to most, that is, not just to Duffy. Anna May Beeston, author of nigh on a dozen brick-thick airport paperbacks and a regular on the chat shows. She is accompanied, escorted rather, by a dis-organised personal assistant – publishing's equivalent to a lady-in-waiting, for the likes of Anna – clutching a batch of what looks like publicity bumph.

'Anna! It's been years!'

She gives him a tentative do-I-know-you smile.

'Chris Duffy. We met at the Ilkley Festival, light years ago now.'

She doesn't remember. 'Of course.'

'I was with the late Anthony Burgess.'

'Poor Anthony.'

Poor Anthony bollocks. She hadn't ever set eyes on him until Duffy introduced them. She was a one-novel wonder in those days, glam already but all fur coat and no knickers. Now she was all fur coat and knickers to match, he shouldn't wonder.

'We all did a book signing at the Crescent Hotel.'

'The Crescent Hotel!'

'He had the paperback of *A Clockwork Orange*, you had *Caesar's Mistress* and I'd just brought out *Razzle-Dazzle!*'

'*Razzle-Dazzle!* What a very good memory you have!'

Well, yes. It was his own sodding book, wasn't it?

'And wasn't it filmed?'

No, it sodding wasn't, because they were too busy filming bastardising *Caesar's Mistress*. Jean Simmons. Made Anna May Beeston's name for her.

The sidekick, or whoever she is, tugs a briefcase out of the limo and allows her armful of bumph to brim over on to the pavement. Duffy helps her scoop it up. She favours him with an engaging grin. Inviting. Promising?

'Oh, this is Lizzie, who's come down to look after me,' says Anna May, obviously for something to say while her chauffeur and the hall porter retrieve her baggage, enough of it for a month's stay, from the boot. Matching pigskin, still newish. Success has yet to scuff her suitcases.

'Dizzy Lizzie,' quips Duffy with oafish gallantry. Lizzie, still unsure whether he's a somebody or a nobody, grins again, but warily this time.

'Are you speaking?' he asks Anna May Beeston. 'Of course you are, obviously. When?'

'Pavilion Theatre, tomorrow afternoon.'

'I'll be there.'

Dizzy Lizzie chips in. 'You'll be lucky, if you don't have a ticket. It's booked solid.'

''Fraid so,' says Anna May.

'Friends in high places,' says Duffy enigmatically. The

cow could have invited him in, couldn't she? Here's my card, she could have said, ask for me at the stage door. Not that he has any intention of going anywhere nearer the Pavilion Theatre than the Pavilion Arms. 'Otherwise,' he adds, 'maybe we can meet up for a drink before you go back.'

'Let's do that.' With a not-if-I-see-you-first smile, Anna May air-kisses her way into the hotel, pursued by Dizzy Lizzie, scattering papers. As she moves into the foyer, Duffy distinctly hears her mutter: 'Now who the *fuck* was that?'

Duffy resumes his stroll along the seafront. Council lorry crews are unloading and stacking crowd barriers to line the route of what, he now dimly recalls from previous years, will be this afternoon's Carnival Collective procession that kicks off the Festival, and features a mobile samba workshop. He must remember to be somewhere else.

Soon he's at the door of the Jackdaw, typical of the pocket-sized pubs still to be found by the score in Brighton. But with the interior of a drinking barracks. Brass, red plush banquettes and bevelled glass, it was. Now it's formica and video games, like a seaside caff. They're all going the same way. So why does he come here? To avoid people. There's always someone to avoid in Brighton.

He's the first in. It was going to be a Guinness to kick the day off but he opts for a large vodka, a chaser after his breakfast miniature. He needs it.

Anna May bloody Beeston. How old is she by now? Sixty? Ish. About the same age as Duffy. She's worn well.

Facelift? And how many books is it so far? At least ten, got to be.

Duffy looks back on that night at the Ilkley Festival thirty-odd years ago and wonders where half his three score and ten went while Anna May was poncing around the world writing her blockbusters.

The Golden Mile: he knocked that off in three months after sobering up when the publisher's advance on *Razzle-Dazzle* was gone. Now can't even remember what he did with the manuscript after it was returned for the sixth time. Could be his ex-wife Mags took it when she buggered off, although Christ knows why. Actually, she didn't so much bugger off as not come back. He barely remembers her – he was pissed when he married her and pissed when she left. Actress. Met her in a pub. Ingénue at that time, playing maids and daffy girlies in weekly rep. Season ends, she went off to join a tour of some grotty detective play or other. She would have gone anyway: good in bed, but both started from the disadvantage that they didn't like each other.

Divorced now, or is he? He calls her his ex-wife but he's not at all sure that she is. He recalls signing some papers but he can't remember what was in them, except that they looked legal. He won't be repeating the experiment so it doesn't matter.

He does owe her one favour, though. There's a drink in it for Mags if he ever sets foot on her again. He came down to Brighton looking for her because he'd heard she was playing the Theatre Royal and he wanted to know how he stood with her. As it happened, he'd got the week wrong – the company had been and gone by the time he reached Brighton. But he liked it here, so much that he never went back, except to pick up his gear. Brighton had an air about it, and it wasn't just the sea air. It was a vague feeling of criminality – the way the little side-street pubs fell silent when you walked into one and they didn't know you – yet with the reassurance that you couldn't be arrested for it. As someone had written, Brighton had the air of having been invited to help the police with their enquiries.

Then there was Jackie, picked up in the Crown and Two Chairmen – where, Duffy sometimes wondered, did teetotallers meet their opposite numbers? – and Brighton took it from there. The antiques racket, Jackie pisses off to Worthing with a fellow-dealer who knows the business better than Duffy – and he takes up with Maureen, picked up in the Whip Tavern. The passing show. Story of his life.

His life. What did he do with it? Where did he leave it, in which cloakroom? Tried a bit of journalism, sold a piece here and there, never followed them up, he's not a journo, he's a fucking writer. One or two short stories, no market for them these days.

Lilliput, Penguin New Writing, the old *London Magazine*, that's when Duffy should have been around, with Mister William Sansom, Mister Laurie Lee, Mister J. Maclaren-Ross, that class of talent, he could have taken them on. That would have shown the buggers.

Television he's tried to crack into. No chance. Writers, producers, directors, all in one another's pockets. Back-scratching. Duffy knows this for a certain fact, from a bloke he met in the Volunteer, intelligent bloke, critic on one of the local weeklies, who'd explained to him the impossibility of selling anything either to the Beeb or the Network. All sewn up.

So what next? Time moves on, frighteningly so. But Duffy has his plans. One of these days, he will get the bastards.

Another familiar figure, or rather a familiar voice, from within the womb-like recesses of the tiny pub. It has only just gone opening-time: he had thought he would have the place to himself.

'. . . I went through the war down here, when I was a girl. People forget that, they forget it because they weren't here, but I was. I went all through it. So don't talk to me about the Blitz because we had it all. You wouldn't know an incendiary if it came up and bit you, would you, but we had an incendiary right through our ceiling, when we were living in the Montpeliers, and that's how I come to be living where I am now. Because I moved to the Brunswicks and went into service, which is what I'd been doing for someone else when I was in the Montpeliers. So course, when she got married and moved across to Sheridan Square, she took me with her. Cook-general, it was called in them days. But then we had words and she wanted me out but I wouldn't go, not me, with what I knew, and she couldn't make me, not without she went to a tribunal . . .'

Duffy, who avoids Olive and shuts his ears to her ramblings when he is able to, hadn't realised that she goes so far back in Maureen's life. Interesting. Does she know what he's looking for? She knows something Maureen didn't want her to know, that's for sure. Could be worth having a quick mosey round her room, if he could stand the stench.

She chunters on. '. . . The rent she has the nerve to charge, I should be the one going to a tribunal. The social services say I don't have a case, but what do they know, they're chits of girls, they know nothing . . .'

She can go on in this vein for hours. She isn't talking to anyone in particular – there's no one in particular to listen to her, the landlord having prudently retreated to the other bar. Duffy used to think she spoke to someone in her head but now he's not too sure, it's more probably just a stream-of-consciousness diarrhoea.

She has a glass of Guinness at her elbow and two plastic carrier bags, probably crammed with rubbish, at her feet, which are clad in old tennis shoes. A man's soup-spattered corduroy waistcoat over a shapeless rag doubling as an ankle-length dress, and the trademark greasy headscarf Olive is never seen without, complete this portrait of a Brighton lady, the lines on her face entrenched with grime like a miniature allotment. Duffy has long thought that Olive is practising to become a bag lady.

He has never seen her in the Jackdaw before, not that he crosses the Hove border all that much himself. Usually, this time of day, she is to be found in the Pineapple, just off Sheridan Square. Barred, probably. Olive tends to get barred from most places, sooner or later.

Not that she makes all that much of a nuisance of herself, provided you don't catch her eye, which Duffy is careful never to do.

He realises, however, that her next rambling mono-
logue is directed at himself:

'. . . I shall have to get that lock changed, because it
doesn't work, it never has worked, what's the word I'm
searching for, it doesn't function properly, you turn the
key but it only goes round halfway, it's not good enough.
So if she won't change it I shall have it done myself and
take it off the rent, see what she makes of that. Then he
won't be able to get in, prowling around whenever I go
out . . .'

The malevolence of her glare, reflected in a Bass
Red Label mirror, can only mean that she is talking
about Duffy. Silly old bat, he has never set foot in her
room. Yet.

But if he hasn't, who has? Who else but Mickey
Daniels? Looking for what? Anything he can lay his
hands on, Duffy shouldn't wonder.

'. . . He thinks I don't know he comes in but I do
know, oh yes, I know all about it. Same as he'll know
all about it, one of these fine days. Because I shall get
the police in if it doesn't stop . . .'

Duffy doesn't rise to the bait. He reckons he's not
intended to, anyway. By muttering away to herself with
the subjects of her complaints always in the third person,
she deflects any possibility of debate, which probably
gets her barred from fewer pubs.

He could murder another vodka but he can hold
out for five minutes. Duffy drinks up and slinks out
past Olive, keeping his eyes firmly on the fake parquet
linoleum.

3

Still killing time, while reflecting that it would have died a natural death anyway if he'd simply stayed in bed for a couple more hours, Duffy next makes his way through the straggling street circus to the foyer of the Brighton Dome.

Nothing much will be going on. Late tonight it will be the venue for the Festival Club – 'a great place to meet your friends after the show, catch up with the Festival gossip and rub shoulders with visiting artists,' according to the brochures. Meaning, as translated by Duffy, riff-raff welcome. But talking of rubbing shoulders, he should be in with a chance of rubbing them with the likes of Dizzy Lizzie or her equivalent minder looking after some other writer or visiting fire-eater. Even at his age, you never knew your luck – some of these lit-chicks fancied the older man. Although he cannot bring to mind the last occasion upon which one did, even when he was a less older man than he is now.

Meanwhile, he is merely sussing the place out. The foyer is not, at this time of day, a hub of activity. There are one or two writers or wannabe writers, bearded buggers as Duffy classifies them whether they sport beards or not, hanging about reading noticeboards in the hope of spotting a free party.

He recognises only one of them – David Somebody, if that's his name. Not David, Donald. Runs, or ran, a television arts programme out of Manchester. Never made it to London. Duffy was on his show when *Razzle-Dazzle* came out. Clearly now demoted to radio, he is traipsing about with a huge out-of-date tape recorder, looking for someone to interview. Duffy nods fawningly. Donald Somebody looks straight through him. Fuck him.

Duffy doesn't know why he has come. He loathes the writing scene, hates most writers, good, bad or indifferent. Always has done ever since he read that Kingsley Amis loathed practically all of them.

He especially has it in for Hemingway and Saroyan, dating back to his boyhood when, with an effort, he gave up writing in slavish imitation of the pair of them. Engraved on his mind is a *New Yorker* profile by whoever the hell it was, which he read in the Blackpool Public Library reading room when such an institution still existed. Pretentious prat that so-called Papa Hemingway was. A passage sticks in Duffy's mind:

'I started out very quiet and I beat Mister Turgenev. Then I trained hard and I beat Mister de Maupassant. I've fought two draws with Mister Stendhal and I think I had an edge in the last one. But nobody's going to get me in any ring with Mister Tolstoy unless I'm crazy or I keep getting better.' Mizz Lillian Ross, that's who the interviewer was. She must have got it down on tape.

Wandering aimlessly about the foyer, and now like everyone else scrutinising posters and notices for want of anyone to speak to, and with no one in the sparsely-occupied space exhibiting any desire to speak to him,

Duffy is stopped at last by a busy-looking, bossy-looking, plumpish young woman he recognises as one Pol Crosby, and who recognises him. With a screech of relief:

'Cliff!'

'Chris. Hello, Pat.'

'Pol.'

Yes, he knows that. Trick of his: always match a wrong name with a wrong name. He remembers her from a couple of years back. One of the Festival organisers.

'You may be just about to save my life. Do you know Moss Cody?'

'Of.'

One of the bearded buggers, although from the photograph on the poster advertising his gig he appears to be himself non-bearded. But looks as if he has in the past sported or may in the future sport a beard. Writes cutting-edge short stories, so Duffy has read, although he has never read any of the stories themselves. Won some memorial prize a year or so ago. Bighead, by the sound of him. Insufferably young.

'He's down for a one-to-one with Jeff Royce at the Corn Exchange tomorrow lunch, full house. But Jeff can't get down – wife ill or some such feeble excuse.'

Jeff Royce. Lit crit on one of the broadsheets. Bearded bugger.

'And you want me to stand in?'

'Do you think you could? There's a drink in it. I know it's short notice.'

'But I haven't read his new one.' Didn't even know he had a new one.

'I'll bike it over to you.'

'Can do,' says Duffy. But wishes he couldn't. In the world he would prefer to inhabit, Moss Cody would be interviewing him, not he Moss Cody. 'And after the success of *Razzle-Dazzle* . . . ?'

'After the success of *Razzle-Dazzle* I had something of a fallow period. Follow that, as the saying goes. So I held back, until the right idea came along . . .'

If only.

He meanders on around the foyer and presently, in an alcove, comes across Donald Somebody, fiddling inefficiently with his tape recorder as he interviews some female critic or other, an American academic of the worst sort, about some book or other Duffy has never heard of.

Lest he be accused of eavesdropping, he stares fixedly at a poster for a guided tour of the Brighton Ghost Walk ('Lamplit stroll featuring local close encounters with the spirit world recounted in vivid detail'), while the American harridan responds to Donald Somebody's plodding interrogation in a voice like fingernails scraping glass.

'. . . But on balance, with the qualifications you've mentioned, Helen Ghastly-Boring' – that can't be her name, but it is what it sounds like, or anyway how Duffy chooses to translate it – 'you thought he just brought it off?'

'Just brought it off but I have to say I did have a prablem with the ending. The way he ties up all the loose ends – I guess that kinda worried me . . .'

Silly cow. Problem? How the hell could anyone be

worried, for God's sake, about the ending of a novel? Did she think it might explode in her face?

Duffy finds himself wondering if she's married, or has a live-in lover in a New York loft. 'What's bugging you, sugar? Can't sleep?'

'No, honey, I guess I'm worried about that novel I've been reading. I just can't buy the way he ties up his loose ends. Call me a fussbudget if you like.'

'C'mon, sugar, let's talk this through . . .'

Disgusted, Duffy wanders away as Donald Somebody begins to ask 'Just how serious' something or other is. The bar isn't open yet, which probably accounts for the paucity of bearded buggers. Duffy is about to vote unilaterally in favour of a quick one at the Cricketers' Arms on the slow drift home to service Maureen at lunchtime, when he is approached, accosted he would say, by a middle-aged, hopeless-looking man in a dandruff-flecked black suit, shiny with age.

'Mr Duffy?'

Yes? Who's this bugger, then? Bailiff? Debt collector?

'Mr Chris Duffy?'

'That's me. How can I help you?'

'Gregory Coates.' He declares his identity as if it should mean something to Duffy. Perhaps it should – how would Duffy know? He smiles glassily. The man could be a publisher, TV producer, somebody, anybody, nobody.

Gregory Coates digs into a shabby, cardboard-looking wallet but can find only a dog-eared visiting card which he produces in error. 'Terence P. Warmby. Articles. Journalism. TV scripts.'

'Beg pardon, I don't seem to have one of my own cards, they go like Smarties around here, let me introduce myself, Gregory Coates.'

'Yes, you said,' says Duffy, not disguising his mystified expression.

'You wrote a book called *Razzle-Dazzle*.'

Oh, Christ, he's a solicitor's clerk. With a writ for libel. After all these years – isn't there a statute of limitation or something?

'I did, yes?'

'I just wanted to say, Mr Duffy, that speaking as some-one born and bred in Lytham St Anne's, *Razzle-Dazzle* is the best novel about Blackpool I've ever come across.'

Apart from *Hindle Wakes*, thinks Duffy, there haven't been all that many. Still, he can always do with praise. It doesn't often come his way.

'You're very kind. Thank you.'

'What I'm wondering, Mr Duffy, is whether you're represented at this present moment.'

Represented? Oh, by a literary agent. 'Not solely,' he says airily. 'In fact . . .' He lets his 'in fact' waft away in the ether, to suggest that he's been through agents like a hot knife through butter, but is still consider-ing offers.

'Because I should be happy to take you on,' pursues Gregory Coates. 'We do have a pretty full stable, but if you chanced to have anything in the pipeline . . .'

'I do have one or two projects in the pipeline, as it happens,' says Duffy grandly, but decides perhaps he ought to be playing hard to get. 'But who else do you represent?'

'Oh, my goodness,' sighs Gregory Coates in a where-should-I-start tone. 'You'll have heard of Xenis Lockworth, the cookery writer?'

Never heard of her. 'Xenis Lockworth, oh yes.'

'She has her own TV spot down here on the south coast. Or did. She's going to be very big. Really zany character. Then there's who?'

'I don't know – who?' asks Duffy helpfully.

'Terry Warmby.'

'Terry Warmby. Do I know the name?'

'Only if you're into chess. He does a syndicated column in some of the regional evenings. I keep telling him if he'd lower his sights into draughts, I could probably get him a spot in one of the Saturday tabloids, but will he listen?'

'Who else have you got?' asks Duffy.

'Sam Rochester?'

'Sam Rochester,' echoes Duffy, as if expected to know who Sam Rochester might be when he is at home.

'Very promising travel writer. Hasn't quite cracked it yet, but he will, he will. His gimmick is that while he's always about to set off, he never actually goes anywhere.'

'Novel,' says Duffy politely. 'And must keep down the expenses.'

'It is novel,' says Gregory Coates, skimming over the wisecrack. 'But he does need someone to lick it into shape. Now I don't know whether you ever do any editing work . . . ?'

Christ, what kind of hack does this bastard take him for? Though on the other hand, he is volunteering to become his agent. 'Tell you what,' says Duffy cautiously. 'Why don't we have a drink?'

'Why not indeed, Mr Duffy?' Do proper literary agents call people Mr Duffy? It should be Chris old man by now, surely. 'Where are you staying?'

'I live here,' says Duffy with that proprietorial pride of resident Brightonians.

'Ah. Then you'll know Pier Lodge, where I shall be until Tuesday.' One of those grotty private hotels off the seafront. He makes it sound like the Royal Albion. 'The public rooms aren't up to much, but if you're near at hand perhaps I could drop in on you one evening.'

No way. Duffy does not have the facilities to entertain callers. For one thing, only one glass. 'Or why not a swift one now – as good a time as any?' he suggests.

Gregory Coates shoots back a cuff to reveal a non-existent watch. 'Ah, I'm just that little bit pressed for time just now.' Meaning, Duffy guesses, he hasn't got any money. 'But we're bound to bump into one another over the weekend.' When he will have borrowed the price of a drink from either one of his two protégés.

They exchange telephone numbers and Duffy continues his perambulation of the foyer, tolerably pleased. So maybe Gregory Coates isn't a top-drawer agent, maybe he's a bottom-drawer agent, but at least he's an agent. Duffy can imagine the note-swapping session with some fellow-scribe here at the Festival Club later tonight: 'I've switched, actually. To Gregory Coates Associates – have you heard of them? You will.'

He moves on. Donald Somebody, having squeezed what neurotic juice he can out of the sleepless and, it seems to Duffy, anorexic and near-demented American critic, is wandering about with his tape recorder, seeking fresh bait.

He still ignores Duffy. Duffy, for his part, ignores him. He fixes on a bearded bugger who clearly recognises him from somewhere or other.

Or thinks he does. To Duffy's surprise, the bearded bugger produces an autograph album with pages of heliotrope, pink and primrose.

'Would you mind?'

'Not at all.' How long since Duffy last did this? 'To?'

'Oh, just put to Trudi, with an i. Girlfriend.'

Duffy scribbles his name as if he does it a dozen times a day, and the dedication to Trudi. The man looks at it blankly.

'Oh. So you're not John Braine?'

'John Braine's dead.'

'Is he really?'

'Has been for a good many years.' By way of consolation Duffy, who has never ever met John Braine, adds: 'I knew him, of course.'

The disappointed bearded bugger, now clearly simply a punter who shouldn't even be here, asks in his autograph-hunting way: 'What was he like?'

'I went fifteen rounds with Mister Braine,' says Duffy magnanimously. 'I was in the ring with Mister Sillitoe and Mister Barstow and we went to a draw but with Mister Braine I won on points . . .'

He becomes aware of subdued giggles at his elbow, and it is Dizzy Lizzie. He is also aware that he has lapsed into a pseudo-American accent, which he is prone to do when he goes into Hemingway mode. He must do somebody else. Mister Amis Senior. Or Mister John Braine, seeing that this bearded bugger seems to think that's who he is.

She's with, or is being joined by, Donald Somebody, who on this occasion condescends to acknowledge Duffy with a nod, only because Dizzy Lizzie has acknowledged him first.

'So where's her royal highness, Liz? She knows I want her in the Old Market at nine tomorrow, doesn't she?'

'She'll be there. I haven't got her time-sheet, David. Is it radio or telly?'

David Somebody after all, then, not Donald Somebody. Same difference.

'Radio, she'll be relieved to know, so she needn't put the slap on. I've given up the telly.'

Duffy sniggers inwardly. Telly given you up, mate, more like.

'Chris Duffy,' he announces, since Lizzie shows no sign of introducing him. Possibly because she can't remember who he is. She is looking rather fetching in what Duffy, in an unpublished short story, once called a lesser black dress, a phrase that pleased him so much he used it in several other unpublished pieces. It now strikes him that it is not conventional pre-lunch wear. She looks as if she is so anticipating the cocktail hour that she can hardly wait for it.

'And it's Dizzy Lizzie, isn't it?'

'How clever of you to remember my name. Even though it isn't. My real friends call me Busy Lizzie.'

'Busy Lizzie, Dizzy Lizzie, either or. Where's Anna?'

'Annie's having a sleep-in. She's got a headache, poor lamb.'

Duffy thinks he catches a touch of irony in that 'poor lamb' note. 'I expect she can afford the odd headache by now.'

'You know Anna May Beeston, then?' asks Donald Somebody – David Nobody, as he seems to have become – nastily.

Duffy is going to have this bugger. He remembers a catch-phrase of the cocky Denry Machin from Mister Arnold Bennett's *The Card*: 'Yes – do you?' Then he repeats, since his self-introduction has yet to be acknowledged: 'Chris Duffy, my name.'

'Yes.' It could mean Yes, I've heard of you, or Yes, so what? The latter, at a guess.

'I was on your Book Show programme light-years ago, in Manchester or was it Leeds? Before you gave up telly,' continues Duffy with malice aforethought.

Donald Somebody or David Nobody fixes him with a look of deep loathing.

'I remember very well. You were on our Watch This Writer spot. We watched and watched and watched but nothing happened. Writer's block?'

Duffy feels himself flushing. Lizzie permits herself a secret smile.

'Let's just say I'm a perfectionist.'

'Don't be perfect, just get published,' quips David Nobody or Donald Somebody.

Lizzie murmurs viperishly: 'And your next book is in whose catalogue, David? Or is it your first book?'

'I'm working on it,' says the victim lamely. Got the bugger. Good for Busy Lizzie. He plods on, skimming the near horizon: 'Liz, there's someone I very much want you to meet.'

Over her shoulder to Duffy, as she allows herself to be speedily propelled across in the direction of nobody in particular so far as Duffy can see, Dizzy Lizzie asks confidentially: 'Shall you be in the Metropole tonight? Tennish?'

'Should I be?' he asks, quite captivated, as he recognises he's meant to be. 'I think I'm supposed to be here.'

'This could be a better offer,' says Dizzy Lizzie, blowing him a kiss. Bit of a saucebox on the quiet, concludes Duffy. Or is that just her way?

An eventful morning – he thinks he will probably leave it at that. All his life Duffy has thought on and off about keeping a diary. The only reason he hasn't is that the times when he's most felt like getting down to it have happened to have been seriously fallow periods in his career. But this would have been as good a day as any to start, if only he had the right kind of squat spiral notebook the task calls for:

'Friday a.m. To the Festival Club in the Brighton Dome foyer. Usual hangers-on but bumped into Pol Crosby who wants me to come to her rescue by interviewing some squirt of a young writer at the Corn Exchange. Peanuts, but worth doing on you-scratch-my-back principles.

'Met David or Donald Whatever his name is, who used to fancy himself as a TV arts personality in Manchester.

How are the lowly fallen – he has now re-launched himself as a radio personality, which is more his mark.

'I also seem to have acquired a new agent, one Gregory Coates. Don't know whether he's up to it, but if anything should turn up on the Maureen front – I shall sound her out this afternoon, after softening her up first – we can try him out on that. Meanwhile, the delicious Dizzy Lizzie has been making distinct kittenish sounds . . .'

And so, via the quickest of quick ones at the Cricketers' pub, to bed.

4

The quick one at the Cricketers' having expanded into the dawdling three, Moss Cody's new opus has already been biked round to him by the time he gets home. What it is called he still has no idea, for he has yet to open the Jiffy bag containing it, and this he has no intention of doing until tomorrow, Saturday.

Last things last is Duffy's motto, or one of them. If he opens the Jiffy bag now, conscientious bugger that he is, he will only start leafing through the swining book, and if he is not mistaken, that muffled thud he can hear from above is the sound of broom-handle on floorboards telling him that Maureen awaits his presence.

No, what he'll do is what he always somehow manages to do on Saturday morning, and that's have a breakfast croissant and espresso at what used to be one of the little pubs in Church Street, now made over as a coffee shop called the Trois Mages, pretentious student-type buggers sipping skinny lattes and smoking roll-ups, and gut this Moss What's-his-bloody-name's book before going across to look over the stall and check that Eggo has got everything up and running.

Doesn't intend to read it, of course, not Duffy – he's done this stint before, once or twice, when someone's let them down, and he can do it on his head. No, no, it's not his bloody book, so why should he do the bloody work? The drill is to read the blurb, read the author biog, skim through a few pages and wing it.

So, Moss Cody, why did you decide on the short story as your particular medium? That's if he did. Check. Could be he's written half a dozen novels, and they've fallen like dead pigeons.

And Ross, as you were, Moss, do you find it more difficult or less difficult to compress what you want to say in ten pages, twelve pages, twenty pages, strike out that which does not apply (memo to self: count average pages)? Let the bugger waffle through a dozen questions of that kind, throw it open to the audience, if there is one, and that should fill an hour adequately. Thank you, Moss Cody, for giving us your time, and Moss will be signing his book whatever it's called, in the lobby. Thank you very much. Twenty-five quid, or whatever the sum might be this year, in Duffy's back pocket.

Another thud from the floor above, more prolonged this time, spurs Duffy into action. Tossing the Jiffy bag on his bed as an *aide-mémoire* for the morning, he applies under-arm deodorant and not reluctantly but certainly with no marked enthusiasm, climbs the steep basement stairs up to the ground-floor flat, wondering who Maureen should be today.

Yesterday she was that little actress, could've played the female lead in *Razzle-Dazzle* if it had ever been made. Today, if he keeps his eyes tightly shut, she can perhaps be Dizzy Lizzie.

Duffy wonders if Maureen plays these kind of games herself, and if so, who he? She's always said she fancies the host of that afternoon game show she watches, who is probably as good a candidate as any, although he's gay if anyone asks Duffy.

Still, none of his business. Get on with it. His priority, as well as, it would seem these days, Maureen's own, is to get it over with. She must have been a goer in her day, hence the kinky stuff in the bottom of her wardrobe, but for a long time now you were talking about the overture to the post-coital cigarette.

And the chat.

'You took your time today,' says Maureen at length, referring to his punctuality rather than his performance. 'Did you fall in with the Festival crowd, or?'

This brings Duffy neatly, and at once, to what he means to be the text for the day. Given a fair wind he can be out of here and back in the pub within the hour.

'Yes, met one or two old faces. And,' he adds after a self-important pause, 'I seem to have acquired an agent.'

'An agent, oh yes?'

Does she know what an agent is? She makes Gregory Coates sound like an insurance agent. Not bad casting, come to think of it. 'An agent, yes. He wants to handle my stuff.'

'What stuff? The book you've lost, or the one you crack on you're writing, or?'

'Both.' Duffy doesn't like that 'crack on you're writing' dig – too close for comfort. *Blackpool Rock*, it's called. Crime novel, supposed to be. Too early to say, he's only done twelve pages, at most. Trouble is, Mister Greene got in there first. Why do these sods always have the best ideas?

'And he's thinking of taking a reissue of *Razzle-Dazzle* on board.' Gregory Coates hasn't said so, in as many words, or indeed in any words at all, but if he wants to call himself Duffy's agent, let him get on with it. In fact they could make it a package deal.

'We're making it a package deal,' says Duffy, greatly knowledgeable.

'Package deal? What package?'

'It's the way they do things these days, Maureen. They sell you as a package.'

'You mean like a parcel, or?'

'Something like that. That mysterious book of yours, for instance, Maureen,' says Duffy slyly. 'We could probably throw that in.'

'Throw it in? You make it sound like a.'

'You know what I mean, Maureen.'

Maureen stiffens. Not that she has been exactly unstiffened all afternoon. Something on her mind. 'You're not banging on about my book again, are you? Because if.'

'Maureen, from the little you've told me this could be a very valuable manuscript, considering who you say worked with you on it. All right, it may need editing, but I could help you out there.'

'You've said. But.'

'Think about it, Maureen.'

As far as they ever get.

And now Maureen changes the subject. Or rather, goes off at a tangent.

'Fact is, I *have* been thinking, Chris. Because we've been going on like this for how?'

For how long? Duffy doesn't like to think how long. How long is too long? The whole of his life has that question 'How long?' hanging over it like a fog-bank.

'What are you getting at, Maureen?' As if he doesn't know.

'Whether we.'

The dreaded question.

So if they ever did get married, and this precious manuscript of hers did turn out to have anything going for it, Duffy would be entitled to a fifty per cent cut, wouldn't he? Or would he? He hasn't the faintest idea. Worth half an hour in the reference library, that one. Somebody's Guide to the Law. Married Women's Property Act. But then what if her book turns out to be worthless? As a consolation prize, does Duffy get half the house, and if so how does he persuade her to sell it when she's always said the only way they'll get her out of the place is in a box?

It's not the money Duffy wants, anyway. He has never given a toss about money. It's the glory, that's it. One of his pub pipedreams. 'You know who that was, don't you? Didn't you recognise him – bloke who just went out? Chris Duffy. Wrote that book.'

Aloud he says: 'Let's see how it sorts itself out, Maureen. After all, there's not a lot wrong with the arrangement we've got.'

'That's what you always.'

It's what he'll go on saying, too. Not the marrying kind, Duffy isn't. Anyway, it could be bigamy, for all he knows. He's pretty sure he must be divorced by now, but the life Duffy leads, that's to say half-pissed half the time, you can never be more than half-certain.

Perhaps it's time to move on. Pastures new. He wouldn't want to move out of Brighton, wouldn't need to anyway – Maureen may be a bit of a clinging vine, but she isn't going to come after him with an axe. He can tell her he needs a bit of privacy to be getting cracking on his new book, which is true enough – so he does. It's just that when he's got his privacy – a little flat in North Laine, he's always fancied, over or next door to a little pub – he'll have to find some reason for the pages still to be non-forthcoming. Got to let them stew, that's it. Plus, there'll be some editing of Maureen's book to be done, once Duffy has got his fists on it.

'Maureen—' he begins, putting his arm around her shoulder.

Maureen becomes agitated. Thrusting him away she says imploringly, as if reading his thoughts, 'Oh, you're not going to start again, are you, Chris? Because.'

But it turns out to be a case of crossed wires. What Maureen is alarmed about is not the topic of her book but the off chance of, as she sometimes puts it, Duffy floating a desire for a second helping. Fat chance. These days, he sometimes has trouble enough with the first helping.

And it's Friday afternoon, isn't it? And on Friday afternoons her friend Mrs Cooney from Chilton Court over in Brunswick Crescent, which used to be Maureen's home back when her mum was still alive, always comes over. As today, Duffy has often been pushed out just as

Mrs Cooney was arriving, and the impression he gets is that these are business visits rather than social.

On one occasion, returning briefly to Maureen's flat to pick up his forgotten sunglasses, he caught Mrs Cooney handing over a bulging envelope containing, unless he was very much mistaken, a bundle of used notes. Is she on the game? Bit long in the tooth for it, not much younger than Maureen although still tolerably presentable, but that's the way some of the punters like them. So where does Maureen fit in? Procuress, isn't she? Picks up mugs at those creative writing circles she goes to, chats them up, then sends them over to Mrs Cooney to be serviced. They're a double act.

In due course, even though he may have got a few details wrong, Duffy will marvel at his own perspicacity. But in the meantime the front-door bell is ringing. Gives him the perfect exit.

'I'll let her in,' says Duffy, tugging on his jeans. 'Mebbe see you in the pub later?'

'Mebbe,' says Maureen as she hurriedly dresses. 'Or.'

One thing Duffy likes about Maureen. She's not too fussed about making arrangements. Nor is Duffy. They pen him in.

He goes out to the street door and admits Mrs Cooney who, as always, gives him one of her yes-and-we-all-know-what-you've-been-up-to sideways looks. Does she talk? Who cares? Duffy doesn't have a reputation to lose. What he'd most like is a reputation in the first place.

5

Having let Mrs Cooney into the house, Duffy now finds himself out in the street. Otherwise he would have gone straight down to the flat and been at his desk by now. As things stand, the pub calls. That's how it works out. That's how books fail to get written.

Duffy is keenly interested in other writers' working methods. He once spent two whole days in bed with a bottle of vodka, reading a series of *Paris Review* interviews in which the literary heroes of the day described how they set about getting their words on paper. Mister Saul Bellow, Mister Edward Albee, Mister Pinter. How Mister Waugh wrote his early novels in six weeks flat, how Mister James Jones took two months to write forty pages of *From Here to Eternity*, and Mister Steinbeck had to sharpen a dozen pencils before he could start at all. Mister Arthur Miller. Mister Allen Ginsberg.

Was Mister Patrick Hamilton in there somewhere? Duffy can no longer recall whether it was from the *Paris Review* or Maureen that he learned how Mister Hamilton used to rise at half past six, write exactly fifteen hundred words and then bugger off across to the pub.

Not as bizarre as it at first seems – bizarre, that is, that he could have heard the story from Maureen. Way back, when Maureen was a girl, her mother ran a guest-house in Brunswick Crescent, Chilton Court as it was called, and Mister Hamilton took a room there for a few weeks towards the end of his life. He'd once lived in Hove as a boy, used it as a location in some of his novels, and had a soft spot for the place. Called it Earl's Court-by-the-Sea, apparently, according to Maureen. Once you get her going on Mister Hamilton, there is no stopping her.

When in the right mood, and with a drink in his hand, Duffy is happy to let Maureen ramble on in this way as he tries to fill in the gaps in her disjointed sentences. Duffy has a lot of time for Mister Hamilton. His kind of writer.

Duffy has begun to drift towards the Lanes with the idea of taking a refresher in the Cricketers' or the Colonnade Bar, but the nearer he gets to Bartholomew Square the more irritatingly persistent is the bam-bam-bam of a one-note African drum, played without any sense of rhythm by someone who might just as well be hammering nails. In competition, or rather juxta-position, a Dixieland jazz trio strikes up, and as Duffy crosses Ship Street he is nearly run over by a unicyclist dressed as Charlie Chaplin. The Festival is getting into full swing. There will probably be barbershop-singing waiters. Certainly there will be living statues.

On a whim, Duffy decides to do a U-turn and head for Mister Hamilton's old pub in Hove. Call it a pil-grimage.

Duffy does not as a rule do Hove, never goes further west than the Jackdaw in Waterloo Street, but for Mister Hamilton he will make an exception. Always meant to do it, but Maureen, not a pub-goer in those far-off days, could never remember the name of his local. Somewhere round the back of Brunswick Crescent, she has said. If the area is typical, that should narrow it down to about half a dozen pubs.

With some background knowledge, from the biographies he has read, of Mister Hamilton's taste in pubs, Duffy eliminates the beer-houses and cosy drinking cabins from the list of contenders, and settles for a former gin palace, made over at some time in the Thirties into an urban roadhouse, which with its long, baronial-effect saloon bar could have been the model for that big public house in *Mr Stimpson and Mr Gorse*, where Gorse starts luring that silly widow into his web.

He can imagine Mister Hamilton sitting over there with three fingers of Scotch and his *Daily Telegraph* crossword at a Benares-ware table by that mock Portland stone fireplace housing a winking electric coal-and-log fire and surmounted by heraldic shields.

The landlord, as he clearly must be from his gun-metal arm bands, bow-tie, yellow tartan waistcoat and goatee beard, looks as if he has been running the place for a good long time. In this atmosphere, Duffy reckons a dry sherry would be in order.

'You'll have been here for a while, I imagine,' he says in faux-chatty mode. Duffy is not the chattiest of souls.

Guardedly, in typically Brightonian who-wants-to-know tones, the landlord says: 'Long enough.'

Cut to the chase. 'Tell me,' says Duffy, having offered the landlord a drink which is refused, 'did a Patrick

Hamilton ever used to get in here? Years and years ago?'

'Friend of yours, is he?' asks the landlord warily.

'Was,' Duffy thinks he'd better say. 'He's dead now.'

'Hamilton,' says the landlord.

'Patrick Hamilton. Wore glasses.'

'Hamilton, Hamilton. No, the name doesn't ring bells. What did he do?'

'He was a writer.'

'A writer?' exclaims the landlord with a reaction of half disgust, half incredulity, as if Duffy had given Mister Hamilton's calling as pimp or pederast. 'We don't get writers in here as a general rule. You want to try the Cricketers'. Or there's an Arts Club he might have gone to.'

'I shouldn't think so,' says Duffy.

'So what did he write, if you say he was a writer?'

'Books.'

'They all say that,' says the landlord. 'What might I have heard of?'

What indeed? '*Rope*?' hazards Duffy. Mister Hamilton wouldn't have gone big on that. Nor on the landlord's scornful response:

'That's not a book, it's a film! Hitchcock. Jimmy Stewart and that other one. Hamilton, do you say? Hamilton. What else has he written?'

Duffy skims through Mister Hamilton's credits. *Craven House? The Siege of Pleasure? Slaves of Solitude? Twopence Coloured* – now that has a Brighton background. But the landlord won't have heard of it.

'*The West Pier*,' he suggests, inspired.

'You mention the West Pier,' says the landlord. 'Have you seen it lately? If that's reopened in my lifetime, or in yours, I'm a Chinaman.'

'*Hangover Square?*' tries Duffy.

'Hanover Square? Never read it.' Tired of this literary quiz, the landlord hitches up his metallic arm bands and ambles down the long bar as far as it is possible to go, leaving Duffy curiously deflated.

He knocks back his dry sherry and departs from the pub, its creaking, slowly swinging double doors echoing his dejection.

What is the point of being a bloody writer if forty years on no one has ever heard of you? What's immortality for?

He trudges on along the seafront, but not before venturing into an obscure-looking discount bookshop.

'Have you got anything by Patrick Hamilton?'

'Patrick Hamilton, Patrick Hamilton. Is he that astrologer?'

6

The blur begins here. He remembers going into a pub and asking, perhaps belligerently: 'Have you ever heard of Patrick Hamilton?' Several pubs, that would be. Certainly he remembers riposting 'Fuck you, then,' in one of them, and being asked to leave. Was that the same pub from which he was physically ejected? Difficult to remember – all these bijou pubs look the same.

Duffy would never admit to being drunk. He does not do drunk. But he does recall reading how Oscar wrote to Bosie: 'During all the time I knew you I was never entirely drunk but never entirely sober.' Duffy will drink to that. Today, though, could be the exception. He puts it down to that unaccustomed glass of dry sherry.

There is percussion dancing going on somewhere along the seafront but thank goodness Duffy is not subject to headaches because he has an urgent need of sleep. The stony beach of Brighton is not the most comfortable of resting places, but he is off at once, despite the distraction of a girls' accordion marching band on the promenade above.

He awakens, reasonably refreshed, in a hotel lobby, as it seems to be – the Metropole, he believes, or it could equally well be the Grand, or the Imperial Hotel in Blackpool or, for all he knows, that bloody place in

Dublin, where he recollects once falling asleep in just such a comfortable armchair as this.

He has no idea how he came to be here. This has got to stop. It is what comes of not eating. Or has he in fact eaten? He believes he is experiencing an aftertaste of hamburger or something of the kind, but he has no recollection of one passing his lips. This is the kind of thing that gives amnesia a bad name. Good line, that – he must remember it. But he won't.

Yes, it's the Metropole all right. Now what had Dizzy or Busy Lizzie said about tennish? So wossatigh now? What – is – the time? Jesus Christ, past eight o'clock. In the evening, that would be, it's to be hoped. Yes, because over by the lifts is what's-her-bloody-name again, Anna May Beeston, and women of the class she has chosen to elevate herself to do not wear black cocktail dresses in the morning. And with her is Dizzy Lizzie, Busy Lizzie, whatever she wishes to call herself, and she too has changed from all in black to all in black – servant or secretarial black, some kind of suit she seems to be wearing, and very fetching it is too. And with them both, in a baggy electric-blue suit that could be sharkskin, but no tie, is a publishing bugger as Duffy believes him to be, except he can't remember the name.

He drifts across. There are other faces around the lobby he vaguely recognises, but they are all reruns of those encountered earlier in the day, if it was today, in the Festival Club.

Among them is Donald Somebody or David Nobody, still traipsing about with his tape recorder and now accosting Anna May Beeston while the lift, from its Tinkerbell indicator light, hovers on some far-flung upper floor. 'But just how difficult is it to keep up to your standard of work?'

What a prat. What's she supposed to say? 'Just lately, it's become only three-quarters difficult, but there was a time early in my career when it was 93.5 per cent difficult . . .'

The publishing bugger Duffy knows from somewhere intervenes. 'Anna has no problems in that direction,' he says smoothly. 'We're talking one hundred per cent professional here.' Clearly he has dealt with this percentage bollocks before. And Duffy remembers who he is.

'Maurice Liversedge, isn't it?'

'Douglas Liversedge.'

'Douglas Liversedge. Chris Duffy.'

Dizzy Lizzie, Busy Lizzie, butts in, although not in any bossy kind of way: 'You're in shot, Duffy.'

'In shot? This is radio, isn't it?'

Lizzie corrects herself. 'This is radio. You're in whatever you're in when it's radio. In the way, I think the expression is.'

'Sorry.'

The interview is resumed. The lift descends at last. Anna May Beeston, with Donald Somebody or David Nobody in attendance, dogged by this Douglas Liversedge as he turns out to be, is whisked upstairs. Leaving Busy or Dizzy Lizzie and Duffy down in the lobby as the lift gates close.

'We weren't quick enough,' says Duffy stupidly.

'You weren't quick enough,' says Lizzie. 'One in the bar then no more in the bar, and then we'd better go up before she starts tapping her tiny foot.'

She leads him across to the lounge overlooking the seafront and they take up two basket chairs. Duffy sinks into his with a sigh.

They order champagne by the glass. Duffy doesn't want his. He tips it, none too surreptitiously, into a plant-holder, hoping that Busy Lizzie will be signing the bill, which to his relief she does, at once. It is not so much that his money is running short, because he no longer has any money, as that even his shortage of money is running short. He will have to hope Eggo sells something off the stall tomorrow. Meanwhile, he will just have to drink less. But what the hell, he is drinking less, isn't he?

'You're looking shagged out,' says Lizzie, responding to the sympathy card he has been playing.

'I am. Been a long day.' Duffy would be at the end of his tether if he had ever thought he had even got near the beginning of it. Can his life stagger on like this? It does, that's the trouble.

'Are you coming to the opening?' asks Lizzie. Of the Festival festivities, she'll mean. At the Festival Club. No.

'Speeches,' he says with a shudder.

'I know. Annie's making one. And she does go on a bit, even when she's sober. So not?'

'If you don't mind, I think I'll just sit here and watch the room go round.'

'Hey! That's funnee! Print that! It's goood!'

56

Gushing, but true. It should be – he's used it often enough. But this time he really means it.

Lizzie fumbles in her bag and presses something sharp-edged into his hand. Credit card? No, hotel room card key. Christ.

'I'm next door to Annie. What you need is a quiet lie-down. Come on.'

Christ and double Christ. Meekly, he follows her into the lift and to whatever floor she takes him to. As they get out she points to a door. 'That's me. You, I should say, till I get back.'

The door of the room next to it, suite, rather, is open to a babble of voices. The same gang they saw clustering around the lift downstairs are now clustering here, like wasps, knocking back champagne. Donald Somebody or David Nobody is working the room with his tape recorder. He appears to be addressing the floor waiter: 'But in a post-feminist society, just how seriously are we to take her work? Or is there a conscious irony here . . . ?' Or maybe he thinks he is still talking to the bearded bugger who has just fled to the sanctuary of the bathroom. Before the floor waiter too can make his getaway, Duffy grabs a glass of champagne from his tray, and raises it to Anna May Beeston across the room. She seems half-cut and shows no sign either of recognising him or of having any intention of acknowledging his toast.

Considerably refreshed at the prospect of a quiet lie-down on, or in, Busy Lizzie's bed – and should he get undressed, or would that be presumptuous? – Duffy takes a cautious sip of champagne. He is perking up.

How many hours since he was in bed with Maureen? And how long since he last had two women in the same day? Life can't be all bad.

Donald Somebody or David Nobody has switched his evidently unwelcome attentions, and his tape recorder, to Douglas Liversedge, who seems to be a member of Anna May Beeston's entourage.

'. . . So who's the dark horse at the Brighton Festival, so far as literature is concerned?'

'Is there one?' asks Liversedge unhelpfully.

'It could be me,' thinks Duffy wistfully, loitering as he awaits an audience.

'So no dark horse, Douglas Liversedge, a leading publisher. So just what would you say is the surest recipe for a runaway literary success in today's competitive market?'

'Write a cookery book tied in with your hit television series and DVD,' says Liversedge dourly. 'Or,' he adds, remembering whose champagne he is knocking back, 'be Anna May Beeston.'

'Thank you, publisher Douglas Liversedge,' says Somebody or Nobody, snarling as he switches off his machine, 'for nothing', and wanders across to re-accost the bearded bugger coming out of the bathroom.

Duffy steps adroitly between Liversedge and his escape route leading to Busy Lizzie, who is hovering in the vicinity of Anna May Beeston and a clutch of hangers-on.

'You don't remember me,' says Duffy, having reintroduced himself.

'More people know poor Tom than poor Tom knows,'

says Liversedge courteously, giving Duffy the opportunity to say who he is, if anybody. But the point is
not who Duffy is, it's who Liversedge is.

'You're my publisher,' Duffy points out.

Half-recognition flits across Liversedge's face. 'Chris
Duffy,' he reminds himself. 'Was.'

'Still am, so far as I know,' says Duffy with some
petulance.

'No, I don't mean you, otherwise I would have said,
expressing myself grammatically as a former editor
should, "were",' says Liversedge pedantically. 'If you're
who I think you are, I was your publisher, past tense,
but not any more.'

Duffy will sort out in a moment what Liversedge is
trying to tell him. 'You published my first novel, it was
called *Razzle-Dazzle*.'

'Decades ago. When we had world enough, and time.
I didn't, but my outfit did. About Morecambe Bay,
wasn't it?'

'Blackpool.'

'Blackpool, as it's sometimes called. So what happened to you?'

'What do you mean, what happened to me? I'm here,
aren't I?'

'I mean why did you stop writing?'

'I didn't. If anyone remembers, I wrote a follow-up,
The Golden Mile. You, or your outfit, turned it down.'

'I don't remember it, but I would always turn a follow-
up down, unless it was a book of recipes. You can't go
on writing the same old novel over and over again.'

'Who says it was the same old novel?'

'It sounds like it, let me put it that way.'

'Anyway, why shouldn't I? *She* does,' snarls Duffy, staring malevolently across towards Anna May Beeston. In any case, I may well have something different for you, in the near future.'

'Not for me,' says Liversedge. 'I've moved on from fiction since you were dabbling in it.'

'To what?'

'Biogs. Memoirs. Autobiography.'

'I'll write you one,' quips Duffy. 'Story of my life. So who's doing your fiction?'

'If you need to ask,' says Liversedge with benign unkindliness, 'you're out of the frame.'

He drifts off, or rather in Duffy's opinion slinks off, to join Anna May Beeston. So – writing her memoirs, is she? No chance of her wanting them ghosted, he supposes. He was once on the verge of ghosting the memoirs of a sword-swallower he knew up in Blackpool, but the pair of them were always too pissed.

Tired and dejected again after that encounter, Duffy finds himself standing all alone in a room awash with conversation.

Anna May Beeston's suite has been filling up with freeloaders knocking back a quick one before going on to the Festival Club. The usual suspects, Duffy supposes, but he doesn't recognise any of them. Nor they him, nor do they display any curiosity as to who he might be. It is a melancholy moment, considering that he is an established writer at a writers' festival, where he appears to be having the impact of wallpaper.

Duffy acquires two glasses of champagne from the

cruising floor waiter and steers them over to the corridor door as if waiting for someone to arrive.

'Who's the other one for?'

Busy Lizzie is immediately at his elbow. That was quick. She takes the spare glass, unbidden.

'Oh, this is my Noah's Ark act,' says Duffy with only a touch of bitterness. 'If I only had one glass they'd mistake me for the fucking unicorn.'

'Drink up,' murmurs Lizzie. A soft hand nestles into his. No other word for it. Nestles.

'Beddy-byes,' she whispers.

7

Memoirs. Memories. How long since Duffy last slept in a hotel room? Of his own, that is, discounting scrappy one-night stands up there in Blackpool and down here in Brighton, if that's where he finds himself.

Not that this one is his own, and not that he's any intention of sleeping now. He lies where Lizzie has left him, slumped across her queen-size bed with instructions not to move until she gets back. This is the life all right.

It must have been the Shelbourne in Dublin, when *Razzle-Dazzle* came out and they had him over to do that TV chat show. Luxury, that was – even more luxurious than this place. He still has the book-matches somewhere.

So why did he never write his memoirs? Perhaps he should. That Douglas Liversedge is a contact, maybe he'd want to publish them. Failing which, Duffy now has an agent, when he can remember the bugger's name. Pity he never kept a diary, but there's always *Razzle-Dazzlé* and *The Golden Mile* as source material, he could flesh that out no end.

Deprived childhood he could build on, now that both his parents are long gone. One up, one down in Fleetwood, three to a bed – no, there are still folk doddering about up there who'll remember. All right, terrace end, fish-and-chip suppers, bread and dripping, arse hanging out of trousers, cut to the teenage years. How he was so skint he had to sleep on the beach. Well, he did sleep on the beach once or twice, when he was too pissed to get home. *Beach Bum*, he could call it, a touch of the Mister Kerouacs.

What days, what wasted days. Why did he never write the musical of *Razzle-Dazzle* when he had the chance? Lionel Bart. That Joan Littlewood would have leapt at it in her heyday. Move over, Mister Frank Norman, Mister Brendan Behan. It would have run a year.

The TV series, the film. Albert Finney. An angry young man, that's what he should've been, if he could have stirred himself.

Is that the answer, then – that he just couldn't be bothered? Or that he ran out of things to say? But he had nothing much to say in the first place. He isn't the kind of writer who says things.

The drink? It must take its share of the blame, obviously, but he was drinking when he wrote *Razzle-Dazzle* and he was drinking when he wrote *The Golden Mile*. Then look at Mister Hamilton, Mister Fitzgerald, Mister Chandler.

Indolence, more like. Face it, Duffy, he had every chance. Born at the right time in the right place, right background, right CV of dead-end jobs. They were crying out for his kind of stuff, one time. He could have sold them his used tram tickets. And no use complaining they shut the door in his face. Every door was open to him back then. But he blew it, didn't he?

Reminds Duffy – old joke, he must tell it to Maureen, she'll appreciate it. Skint writer, at long last gets fat commission from *Reader's Digest*. Big payers – all he's got to do is sit down and write the piece and he's in the money. Puts it off, puts it off, puts it off. Finally gets a letter from *Reader's Digest*: Are you going to write that sodding article or not, otherwise forget it. Sends them a telegram: Commencing article as soon as have finished cleaning my tennis shoes.

Duffy has spent four decades cleaning his tennis shoes. All there is to it. No one to blame except himself – though doubtless, by morning, he will have found another scapegoat.

The things he could have done. He drifts into sleep having won the Booker Prize, and awakens who knows how long afterwards with no knowledge at all of where he is. Nothing unusual about that, for all that he never goes anywhere these days. The Clock Tower bell near by sounding the half-hour gives him a clue. The Hotel Thing. Metropole. But what it does not tell him is who that is breathing so heavily on the adjoining pillow. Not Maureen, that's for sure – wrong scent. Thingy. Dizzy Lizzie. Busy Lizzie.

So how the hell did she get in here? Of course, it's her room, isn't it? Must have two keys. In the sea-light filtering through the net curtains, he sees that she is naked. So, come to that, is he, except for his Y-fronts. Did he undress himself? Has no recollection of doing so. Who undressed whom? An imperfect picture shimmers into his mind, like a badly-focused television screen, of her tugging his jeans off. There they are down on the floor. So then what?

Nothing. Both too rat-arsed. Hence the retention of his underpants and, as he now notices, his socks.

No time, though, like the present. Duffy is stirred into stirring. Lizzie does not stir. She is spark out.

Undeterred, or not very much deterred, he proceeds to grope her in an increasingly uncouth manner, angry both with himself and her, particularly her for behaving like a rag doll. Eventually, without awakening, she begins to respond, but intuitively rather than consciously. She is on autopilot.

By the time he has had his way with her – the only way he can phrase it – she is yet to wake up. He wonders if technically this could have been rape. Feeling somewhat like what's-his-bloody-name in what-was-it-bloody-called, *The Forsyte Saga*, he rolls over to his own side of the bed.

What the hell is he doing here, anyway?

Sobered up a little by his brief, more or less unilateral bout of sexual exercise, Duffy props up his pillow and backtracks through the evening's activities, accounting for most of his movements, with only one or two blanks, to his satisfaction. So the amnesia is not yet total.

Lizzie's yawning voice: 'Where are you?'

Oh, Christ. Post-coital conversation he can do without. Like attending a post-mortem.

'Here. Next to you,' he stalls.

'Mentally. What are you thinking?'

He gives the hackneyed question as much attention as it deserves. 'About what we've been doing. It was marvellous,' he says mechanically.

'Aren't you supposed to say "How was it for you?"'

'So how was it?'

Now half sitting up herself, she shrugs a bare shoulder. 'It was OK.' Then, injecting something like enthusiasm into her voice, she amends the verdict: 'No, truly, I mean yes! It was great.'

A likely story. 'Why me?' asks Duffy bluntly. This is something he really does want to know.

'Why not?' says Lizzie. 'Because you're here.'

'Yes, but so are a lot of lithe young lads with lean and hungry faces.'

'I'll get round to them. I've got all weekend.'

'Best-sellers, some of them, at half my age. I'm sixty-one years old and haven't published for years. So why me? What's in it for you?'

'Silly question,' says Lizzie. 'It's what I do.'

'What you do. You make it sound like a career.'

'It is, in a way. Now that'll do about me,' she continues briskly. 'Let's take you now. What do you want?'

'I want you,' mumbles Duffy with ersatz sexual hunger.

Recognising this for the twaddle it is, Lizzie continues: 'No, we've done that. What do you really want?'

Jesus God, she's not going to say 'out of life', is she? More or less, she does.

'For yourself. What haven't you done that you should have been doing?'

'Written five more novels.'

'If you needed to do that badly enough,' says Lizzie, 'you would have done it by now.'

'So what should I have done instead?'

'I don't know. What *have* you been doing?'

'Fuck-all.'

'We have a writer in our stable who's sweated through twenty-two books in all the time you've been busy doing fuck-all,' says Lizzie. 'And I think you may have the better deal. You're making the mistake of thinking that doing something is superior to doing nothing.'

'That's very shrewd,' says Duffy, without considering whether it is or not.

'Not original,' says Lizzie. 'Now go back to sleep.'

'Thanks. I will.'

But not for long. There is a sharp rat-a-tat on the door.

Lizzie catapults herself upright. 'Christ! What time is it?'

Duffy can just make out the figures on his digital watch. So that wasn't the half-hour when he heard the Clock Tower bell striking. It's only just gone one o'clock. And here was he thinking it must be around fiveish.

The doorknob rattles and a hoarse voice cries from out the corridor: 'Lizzie!'

'Who is it?' whispers Duffy.

'Douglas Liversedge.'

'Tell him to piss off.'

'I can't very well. He's my boss.'

'At this hour? You do night shifts, do you? What does he want?'

'Me. He thinks he has *droit de seigneur*. Besides, I must have asked him up.'

'Christ, Busy Lizzie, you're not into three-in-a-bed, are you?'

'I haven't sunk that low yet! I forgot you were here, that's all. You'll have to hide. No, not in the bathroom – he has a weak bladder. In there!'

Kicking his discarded clothes under the bed, Lizzie shoves Duffy towards the mirrored built-in wardrobe.

'What if he looks in here?' objects Duffy.

'He's not going to pee in the wardrobe, sillee. Anyway, I'll lock it. Move!'

Another tattoo on the door and Liversedge's plaintive voice calls drunkenly: 'Lizzie? What are you doing in there?'

'I'm coming, I'm coming!'

'You can't be coming yet, we haven't even started.'

'Oh, God, he's going to wake up the whole bloody hotel,' says Lizzie agitatedly as Liversedge's dirty laugh resounds along the corridor. 'Get in!'

She pushes Duffy into the wardrobe, throws his trainers in after him and slams the sliding door. The light automatically extinguishes itself and he finds himself in darkness, save for the thinnest blade of light shining through what he imagines must be the keyhole. A click as Lizzie presumably locks him in. Then the sound of the bedroom door opening and Liversedge's thick, aggrieved voice:

'What took you so long?' Then, suspiciously, 'Have you got someone in here?'

'Of course not – what do you take me for?'

'Our Busy Lizzie, that's who I take you for,' retorts Liversedge nastily. Duffy hears the bathroom door creaking open.

'What are you doing – casing the joint?' asks Lizzie.

'If you want to put it like that. All right – whose are these on the floor?'

Oh, Christ, what's he found? 'They're mine,' he hears Lizzie respond calmly.

'But you never wear jeans.'

'I'm not allowed to wear jeans, if you remember, except on Dress-down Friday, but you're never in the office on Friday so you never see me in them. Otherwise I wear them when I'm off, like now. As are they.'

This last remark, needlessly coquettish in Duffy's view, provokes Liversedge to respond, doubtlessly with a leer:

'All right, girlie, let's get down to it. Where's the champagne?'

'I haven't got any.'

'But we always have champagne.'

Always? How often is always, futilely wonders Duffy.

There is a degree of scuffling and shuffling and a soft thudding, consistent with Liversedge shedding his clothes and shoes. Not being a voyeur, even an aural one, Duffy does not look forward to the next ten minutes of grunting, groaning and grinding, or however long it's going to take.

But he is mistaken. It is not the sound of Liversedge undressing but of Lizzie dressing. Not, Duffy hopes, in the jeans she has claimed as her own. That would be taking bedroom farce too far.

'Come along,' he hears her say firmly. 'There's champagne downstairs.'

'But we've only just come up. What's wrong with room service?' bleats Liversedge.

'Takes too long at this hour. We'll have a glass downstairs and then we can bring a bottle up.'

Rightly taking this as a stage direction to himself, Duffy waits for the bedroom door to open, and then close again, followed by the shuffle of retreating footsteps. He waits two minutes to make allowances for Liversedge's weak bladder and an emergency pit-stop back to the bathroom, and then in the pitch dark he tugs at the wardrobe's sliding door.

The silly cat has forgotten to unlock it.

Oh, no, she can't have done. Yes, but he would have heard the click. There was no click. And the door won't budge.

If Duffy had a mobile phone he could have paged the stupid bitch down in the hotel bar and brought her up to the rescue. But he doesn't have a mobile and if he did it would be in his discarded jeans by the bed.

Plan B could be to break the wardrobe door down. But Duffy has enough experience of life to know that breaking doors down is not as easy as in rented videos.

Plan C is to wait patiently in the dark for Lizzie's and Liversedge's return. Sod that – they could be hours. And unlike her supposedly incontinent lover, he is in urgent need of a pee.

Plan D is another B-movie scenario: grope around in the dark until he has found the lock, the guiding thin beam of room light having been extinguished upon

Lizzie considerately switching it off on her way out, then coax the key out of it – that's if the key is still in it, and not in that silly cow's handbag – on to a sheet of newspaper or something, and pull it gently under the wardrobe door.

He sets about this operation in earnest. At least it will pass the time.

There are no sheets of newspaper to hand. There should be some lining paper in the wardrobe's shirt drawers, but there isn't. The wardrobe, indeed, except for some outer clothing on clanking hangers, seems empty. Doesn't she wear underclothes? Given her emerging track record, probably not.

There could be, from his small experience of first-class hotels, a plastic laundry sack somewhere. He fumbles about in the blackness and yes, by its clammy feel, this seems to be one.

He now fumbles further along the wardrobe's sliding doors until he locates what could very well be the keyhole. All right: he smooths out the laundry sack and feeds it out under the wardrobe door so that when he pokes out the key with his ballpoint pen it will fall down on to the spread-out laundry sack, with any luck, which he will then gingerly pull back into the wardrobe. Locate the key and release himself. Get dressed, then go down and kick the shit out of Dizzy Lizzie.

He has successfully spread the plastic sack under the door and is less than successfully probing what he believes to be the keyhole with his ballpoint pen when the wardrobe door glides soundlessly open. Its recess is filled with light, and Duffy, naked except for his socks and the trainers he has inexplicably tugged on after they were tossed into the wardrobe by Lizzie, finds himself facing the tape-recorder-toting presence of Donald Somebody or David Nobody.

'Oh, sorry,' says Somebody or Nobody. 'I didn't realise there was a queue.'

8

She is not in the hotel bar, which shows signs of winding down for the night. Still simmering, he makes his way along the seafront and round to the Brighton Dome and the Festival Club. Its elaborately-decorated foyer is buzzing.

Duffy begins to barge his way to where he imagines the bar must be, but before he can get halfway to it, she appears in front of him bearing two glasses of champagne.

'Reciprocation,' smiles Busy Lizzie.

'Thank you for nothing,' snarls Duffy. 'Left to you, I would still be locked in your sodding wardrobe.'

'It doesn't lock, as it turns out,' points out Lizzie.

'So I eventually discovered,' says Duffy. 'But how was I to know that, when the wardrobe door was jammed?'

'I'll complain to the management.'

'I should. You never know who might need to occupy it next.'

Lizzie decides to take this with another smile. 'So who let you out? That jerk with the tape recorder?'

'Yes. What was he doing up there?'

'I gave him my key.'

'Why?'

'Really, Duffy, this inquisition!'

Absolutely. None of his business. 'Absolutely,' he says, echoing his own thought. 'None of my business.'

'If you need to know, he's a contact. I hope you didn't leave him in my room, by the way?'

'No, he came down with me. In fact, he's over there.' Duffy nods over a sea of heads towards Somebody or Nobody who, tape recorder on the go as always, is talking earnestly to an astonishingly young-looking man, no more than a youth really, with butter-coloured hair.

'So he is. With the Boy Wonder.'

'Who's the Boy Wonder, then?'

'Not one of ours, unfortunately. Flavour of the month, I gather.'

Doggedly, Duffy returns to his earlier theme. 'So if you didn't want God's gift to broadcasting in your room, why give him your key?'

'House detective are we now?' says Lizzie, bristling. 'He wanted to ring his office.'

'And his mobile was on the blink,' supplies Duffy.

'And his mobile was on the blink. Look, can we stop this? Ten minutes in bed together and you're coming on as if we were an unhappily married couple.'

So she gets garrulous when she's pissed, does she? Duffy unwisely tries a joke. 'Twenty minutes in your wardrobe and I was ready for a divorce. What happened to the other co-respondent? Douglas Liversedge?'

'Called it a night and went to bed.'

'His own bed, I take it?'

Shouldn't have said that – he's exceeded his joke quota already. 'If you've hopes of becoming a stand-up comedian, don't give up the day job.' She stalks off to the bar, having crossly knocked back her champagne.

Nevertheless, despite Lizzie's little tantrum, it has the makings of a jollyish evening. A Dixieland jazz combo, probably the same one he heard hours ago or it could have been days ago in wherever it was, has struck up somewhere. Duffy has got his third wind, or it may be his fourth. He'll give Lizzie a chance to grump herself away from the bar and then fight his way through for another glass.

'Excuse me. Mister Duffy?'

It is the impossibly young man with the flaxen hair. Plus, Duffy notes, what appears to be his school blazer. No, can't be – just a stripy summer blazer, as worn by flavours of the month.

'Yes?' He can only imagine the youth has got his name from Somebody or Nobody, and wants to scrape an introduction to Busy Lizzie. She's too old for him.

'You wrote a novel called *Razzle-Dazzle*.'

Such a respectful voice. 'So I did,' says Duffy, gratified.

'I haven't read it, I'm afraid. It seems to have gone out of print.'

'Probably. Books do. To make way for the newcomers.' That should please the young fellow. He's obviously written one.

'I was trying to get hold of a copy. Because, you see, that was going to be the title of my own novel.'

Cheeky little sod. 'Beat you to it, didn't I?' says Duffy, with just a hint of nastiness.

'Pity. It would have been just right for me.'

'Yes, it's a good title. So what have you called your novel at the death?'

'*To Hell Like Lambs.*'

'Come again?'

'It's a quote. Chesterton. "The folk that live in Liverpool, their heart is in their boots; They go to hell like lambs, they do, because the hooter hoots."'

'You don't sound Liverpudlian,' says Duffy. Public school, more like. Mockney.

'If it comes to that, you don't sound Blackpudlian.'

'I've been down here a long time. Done Blackpool, got the T-shirt. *Razzle-Dazzle* would have been a better title.'

'Yes, I know it would,' says the young blade. 'I was told there was no copyright on titles, but then I was advised that it might cause confusion.'

'Confusion.'

'In the event of your book ever being reprinted.'

He didn't say 'On the back of mine', but the breath of a hint was there. Arrogant young pup. Duffy says: 'So your novel's about Liverpool, is it?'

'Set in Liverpool, yes.'

Resisting the temptation to call the boy 'son', Duffy says patronisingly, 'Don't want to douse your enthusiasm, but hasn't it all rather been done?'

'Set in Liverpool, I said. It's not about Liverpool.'

'So what is it about?'

'Life,' says the boy grandly.

'That's been done too, I think you'll find,' says Duffy. 'But,' he adds generously, 'I wish you the very best of British luck.'

'Thank you, Mister Duffy.'

The splay-footed Pol Crosby has waddled over and is awaiting her chance to collar the Boy Wonder. He hesitates.

'I don't suppose you'd consider donating your title, would you?'

Now if he'd said selling . . . 'Sorry, kid, it's still got mileage in it.'

'I'm going to whisk this young man away, Chris,' says Pol Crosby firmly. 'He's wanted over at the Grand by the *Guardian*.'

'The *Guardian* at the Grand?' scoffs Duffy. 'Contradiction in terms, surely.'

He shakes the young man's hand, with a pang at his own lost youth and those lost interviews with the *Guardian*.

'Don't forget you've got Moss Cody tomorrow lunchtime,' says Pol Crosby as she leads the protégé away.

Moss who? Oh, him. 'I'll be there.'

Lizzie is again at his elbow, again with two brimming glasses of champagne. He notices that in the uncompromising battery of lights set up by a TV crew recording background for tomorrow's late-night Festival roundup, her face looks suddenly lined and tired. Haggard would be the word. At first sighting – was it only this morning? – she had reminded him of a butterfly as she flitter-fluttered into Brighton. Now she is like a butterfly that is turning into a moth.

'Sorry I was a bit ratty just now. One of those days.'

'Yes, I know. I played a small part in it, remember?'

She lets this go. 'So what did you think of the Boy Wonder?'

'Precocious young bugger,' grumbles Duffy.

'He has much to be precocious about. Do you know what he's getting for his film rights?'

'I believe these things when they happen, which they usually don't,' says Duffy sourly.

'Be like that. Don't you want to know about his publishing advance?'

'Not a lot. Oxbridge, is he?'

'Will be, after his gap year in India,' says Lizzie. She sways to the rhythm of the Dixieland jazz outfit. 'He's going to be a rich young man.'

'No doubt.'

'And famous with it. They're calling him the most startling talent to emerge since – oh, I forget when.'

'Last Tuesday fortnight?' suggests Duffy.

'Miaow! He does sound interesting, though – writes in the Scouse vernacular.'

'Been done.'

'Not the way he does it, apparently. The new James Joyce, they're saying.'

'There wasn't a lot wrong with the old James Joyce,' says Duffy, never having got further than *Dubliners* and a few pages of *Ulysses*.

'Wouldn't you have liked to have been a rich young man, Duffy?'

'If I'd wanted to be one, I should have been one,' says Duffy, believing it himself.

'What *do* you want?' asks Lizzie, as tired as he is of Eng Lit, and quite deliberately, as if changing gear, switching to seductive mode. Jesus Christ, does she never stop?

'I'll tell you what,' says Duffy, thinking of the day ahead. 'Could you possibly lend me twenty quid?'

SATURDAY

9

Not a bad house at seven quid a throw. Not packed by any means, but plenty of bums on seats. This Moss whoever-he-is, Duffy will remember his name in a jiff, must have something going for him.

Moss Cody, that's who. But where the hell did Duffy leave his book? It doesn't matter, because the venue will be stacked with copies, but there's a touch of the alcoholic Alzheimer's here that rather bothers Duffy.

He set out with the book, that's for certain. Still in its Jiffy bag. Didn't open it in the Trois Mages where he'd gone for his morning croissant, his Saturday treat, because he got chatting with some bloke at the next table he knows from somewhere. Bloke who runs the Video Exchange, that's who it was.

He definitely had the package when he left the café. Did he? Yes, he did. So round to the Pineapple for a quickie, but he was driven out of the Pineapple, wasn't he, by Olive? Thought she'd transferred her affections to the Jackdaw, he wishes she'd make her bloody mind up. But he still had the package under his arm upon leaving the Pineapple, remembers it, because he had a fag in his mouth and instead of struggling to get his lighter out of his top pocket he stopped on the way out and begged a light from that one-armed news-vendor who always sits by the door.

So far so good. On to North Laines to the stall, where Eggo was drinking tea from a Snoopy mug. Lives on tea, does Eggo. Sycophantic, snivelling leer he has.

'Morning, boss.'

'You said that, Eggo, I didn't.' Duffy noted that the stall was in reasonably good order and scanned the half-literate list Eggo had made of the morning's takings up to now on the back of a Brighton Festival flyer.

'What's this vase, Eggo?'

'Vase, wannit? Japanese, Chinese, looked like. LM/ST – that's £8.50, right?'

'It's £23.90, you stupid berk! Who bought it?'

'That mater yours. Him what goes in the Crown and Two. Lives upstairs from you, doanee?'

Mickey Daniels. 'And you sold it to him for what?'

'Six quid. I went looking for you in the Pineapple to ask what your lowest was, but you wasn't there, boss. He beat me down, dinny?'

Six lousy quid. And Duffy hadn't even known he owned it. It had to be the twin of the one Mickey had carried off from Maureen's flat, otherwise why would he want it?

So now he had the pair. Learn your lesson, Duffy: get rid of Eggo, find someone with half a brain.

Yes, but wait a minute. 'If you sold it to Mickey, what's it doing under the stall, wrapped in last night's *Evening Argus*?' No mistaking it, although he can only see the rim. It was the duplicate of Maureen's Japanese vase.

'He's coming back for it, enny? Got a bitter business somewhere.'

'When he comes back for it, Eggo,' said Duffy, speaking slowly, 'tell him it's sold. Sold, right?'

'He knows that, boss. He's already bought it.'

'Already sold, Eggo. To a previous customer. Give him his money back.'

'Give him his money back? What, his eight quid?'

'Six quid, Eggo, surely.'

'I shudder said six quid, boss.'

'You should, Eggo, you should.'

'What about my commission, then?'

'Take it out of the eight quid.'

So, onwards and upwards. And with the vase under one arm and Moss Cody's book under the other, he headed where? To the Gryphon in Middle Street, tried to, with the intention of leaving the vase with the guvnor until he could get back for it after the Moss Cody gig. But the Gryphon wasn't the Gryphon any more, it's had a makeover since he was last in only a couple of weeks ago, and now it was the Bamboo Bar.

Gay, by the look of the place, or probably would be when it started filling up at night. Yes, it was: bloke in a string vest sidled up to the next chromium stool and ordered a strawberry daiquiri. Asked Duffy if he was down for the weekend. Duffy said no, he lives here. Bloke said how extraordinary they've never met before, but of course this used to be a straight bar. Duffy knocked back his vodka and was off like a bat.

Did he still have the book? Yes. Positive. Did he still have the vase? Yes. No. And he didn't leave it with the guvnor because since the makeover the guvnor wasn't there any more.

Bugger the vase, he'll pick it up later. What did he do next? With half an hour to play with he went across to the Pavilion Arms. Favourite haunt of Maureen's, and there she was, nursing half a Guinness, making an early start of it this morning.

She didn't see Duffy, for the reason that he didn't give her the chance to. Having reached the pub's open door and spotted her, he quickly moved on. Just time to get across to her flat for a quick look-round, having remembered somewhere he hasn't searched – behind the screen that had concealed the vase, the twin of the one he had left in the Bamboo Bar, before it was purloined by Mickey. Mickey wouldn't have noticed what Duffy was looking for, because his greedy eyes had been pegged on the vase.

Nothing. There were one or two other nooks and crannies he could have checked out while he had the premises to himself, but he was jumpy. Maureen always has three glasses of Guinness before lunch but how was he to know that wasn't her third? He abandoned the search.

The quickest of stiffeners at Doctor Brighton's and now here he is at his speaking venue, the Corn Exchange. Minus the package containing whatever-his-sodding-name's book. So he left it in Doctor Brighton's? No, he didn't. He has a photographic image of the thing, where he left it at Maureen's, on her hall table. Shit.

Too late to do anything about it. She must be back home by now. Anyway, he's on-stage in five minutes.

He'll wing it. Think of something. 'Yes, I did drop in, Maureen. Thought you might like to come round and watch me making a prat of myself at the Corn Exchange, then grab a bite of lunch. Did I leave a book at your place, by the way?'

Pol Crosby, waddling up and down on her splayed platform soles outside the stage door, is in even more of a tizz than in the Brighton Dome foyer yesterday.

'Chris, thank goodness, I thought you were dead. Listen, I'm in a terrible fix. I've got myself double-booked – I have to introduce that ex-Minister, you know, the one who wrote *I Did It His Way*, at the Gardner Arts Centre like five minutes ago. Do you think you could be a doll and hold Moss Cody's hand yourself?'

'You mean go on cold?'

'It won't be such an ordeal – it's a good house.'

Duffy shrugs. 'It'll cost you, darling. Where's his biog?'

'There's all you need on the book jacket.'

'So where's the book?'

'I biked it round to you. Didn't you get it?'

'Yes, but I must have left it somewhere.'

Pol, about to clomp into a waiting taxi, shoots him a glance of suspicion. 'You have read it, I hope?'

'Of course I've bloody read it,' bluffs Duffy.

'There's copies out front. I left him there opening the boxes. He's in a filthy mood, sorry to say. Bless him, he thinks I should have done the job for him. So I would have done, if I'd been a human amoeba.'

Duffy takes himself round to the Corn Exchange foyer, where a straggle of punters are wandering into the hall. There are Festival posters and leaflets festooning the place, some of them featuring the youngish, corduroy-clad bearded bugger, as he would be had he not shaved it off or was yet to grow it, who is struggling to rip the masking tape off the cardboard packing case of books stamped with the logo of his publisher.

Duffy introduces himself. Moss Cody grunts. Evidently hand-shaking does not figure in his code of good manners.

'You'd think they'd have someone down here to set up shop,' he grumbles. 'And where am I supposed to sit?'

Dropping his outstretched hand, Duffy happily reflects that he needn't give a toss where the petulant young sod is supposed to sit to sign his books, because as it turns out he won't be signing any. Yanking the tape off the cardboard flaps, Cody prises the case open to reveal its stack of chunky, brightly-coloured books with covers the thickness of plywood, featuring a cartoon depiction of a scarlet-blushing, farting piglet.

Some mistake here. A Scratch 'n' Sniff Book. *Piggy-Pooh's Second Smelly Story. Niff Niff!*

Duffy doubts whether the Piggy-Pooh saga forms a part of the Moss Cody oeuvre.

Cody is already punching the keys of his mobile with the force of a shipyard riveter. 'Jude? Cody. Just what the fuck is going on?'

For the next five minutes Cody paces up and down the foyer, ranting into his mobile. It emerges that forty copies of his own book have been despatched to the Kidz Look-I-Can-Read Fayre in Bournemouth, while he is saddled with the adventures of Piggy-Pooh. Jude, whoever Jude may be, is mortified, but at this late hour, with her author due on the platform, there is nothing to be done about it. She could contact the local Waterstone's, but they would only have five copies, even fewer if by any chance they have already sold one.

Cody flings down his mobile and remembers Duffy as his would-be interlocutor.

'No point in going on with this farce now, chum, wouldn't you say?'

Duffy is not about to be done out of his fee. 'You've got an audience out there. Besides, even if you don't flog any books today, it's all publicity.'

Seemingly seeing the sense in this, Moss Cody suffers himself to be escorted into the hall and along the centre aisle towards the platform. A few heads turn curiously but there is no applause: no one seems any too sure who the pair are. Duffy is not sure that he is sure himself.

They mount the platform. Duffy has the same sensation he has in a recurrent dream where he is walking through the Marina minus his trousers. But he can't pinpoint the source of his anxiety.

Yes, he can. The book he is still holding. *Piggy-Pooh's Second Smelly Story*. He has not got a copy of Cody's book. He cannot remember Cody's name.

Beads of sweat would be appropriate but it is not beads of sweat that Duffy is conscious of. It is beads of vomit in his throat.

All right, he can handle this. Swallow. Breathe. If

necessary, get up and go to the lavatory. They can't arrest you for it. Swallow. Breathe.

It's as good as it's going to get. The sweat now does make a belated appearance, trickling down his throat and into the rim of his shirt collar.

There is some coughing and shuffling. An officious-looking man in a belted raincoat rises from the third row to suggest, in a threatening tone disguised as geniality: 'Ready when you are, Mr Chairman.'

Duffy scrapes his chair nearer Cody's and clears his throat of its residue of phlegm.

'So. Without preamble. Martin.'

'Moss.'

'I should have said Moss.'

'You should, yes. Who's Martin?'

Who indeed is Martin? 'I'm thinking of Martin Amis,' says Duffy ingratiatingly.

This does not go down well with Moss whatever-his-name-is. He snaps: 'Different genre, different generation.' It is not a good start. Get the first question in. Ask him about the fucking book. That gets them going.

Title?

Oh, Christ. It's not that he can't remember, it's that he forgot to ask.

Wing it, then.

What's this bugger's name again?

'So.' He leers conspiratorially at Moss Martin, not Moss Martin, Moss Cody, to suggest that they're in this cock-up together. 'So you've written this book, Moss. *What's the next step?*'

Moss Cody transfixes Duffy with a look of total

contempt. He quarter rises and glances offstage in the hope of rescue. Someone to take his arm, or more preferably Duffy's arm, and lead him gently away with the announcement that owing to the Chair's indisposition the interview has to be foreshortened and refunds will be available at the box office.

There is no one there.

'The next step,' says Moss Cody with a heavy sigh, 'is to publicise it.'

Which he proceeds to do, and at length. This is fine by Duffy. He nods and grimaces like a TV interviewer doing cutaway reaction shots. This should be good for seven minutes at least. In that time he can think of another question.

How come a prat like you is able to get published?

Perhaps not. So why did you choose the short story as a medium rather than, say, sauce-bottle labels? For it does emerge that, as suspected, Cody is a short-story writer. By way of his act he seems hell-bent on synopsising each story in turn. The book, it seems, is called *Twelve Tales and Another*, presumably making thirteen in all. So far, ten minutes in, he has accounted for only three.

What is also beginning to emerge is that while this Moss Cody may or may not be a good writer, he is a rotten speaker. As he plods on, his audience is restless. There is much coughing and buttock-shifting. The man in the belted raincoat looks at his watch and shakes it. If the stupid sod isn't careful he will be getting the slow handclap.

Duffy awaits his opportunity. The bugger has to

breathe some time. At the first pause he is in like a rat in a corn bin.

'But how would you place your work in comparison with other masters of the genre?'

'I never make comparisons, especially since my stories are so disparate.' Yes, they all say that, get on with it. 'Now the one I was just coming to, *Money Still for Tea* . . .'

No way. 'If you had to go fifteen rounds with one of your near-contemporaries, who would you have against the ropes? Mister Amis? Mister Wilson?'

'We've done Mister Amis. Which Mister Wilson did you have in mind?'

Jesus Christ, how many Wilsons were there? Duffy has been thinking, insofar as he has been thinking at all, of Angus Wilson, the last Wilson he has read, but he must be getting a bit old hat by now. What about what's-his-name, Colin Wilson? Big name in the late Fifties. *The Outsider*. Duffy remembers being jealous of the furore. Does he write short stories?

He plays safe. 'Any Mister Wilson you care to nominate.'

Duffy cannot be doing with much more of this. While his interviewee begins to ramble on about A.N. Wilson or possibly Edmund Wilson, he mouths that he is going to see if Moss Cody's books have turned up, and stumbles out to the wings. With his back to the stage, he takes a deep swig from the quarter-bottle of vodka he has had the forethought to buy on the way here. Furtively he glances behind him to see if Moss Cody's eyes are upon him. They are. Fuck him. Duffy drains the quarter-bottle and saunters, as a cover-up from staggering, back to his place.

The speaker is hopeless, and knows it. He is agitated, his right knee jerking up and down convulsively. Sitting, Duffy finds himself replicating these involuntary spasms, but with his left leg, so that he and Cody look as if they are working the treadles of a battery of sweatshop sewing machines. Time to get a grip on the situation.

He cuts across Cody's burblings. 'That's all very well,' he says firmly, 'but is Angus Wilson read much these days, if at all?'

'We're not talking about Angus Wilson,' snarls his irritated guest.

Duffy plods on. 'Short stories, we're talking about, cock. Angus Wilson wrote some of the best, or didn't you know that? *Such Darling Dodos.*' He continues carefully, forbidding his voice to slur. 'But I have to tell any of these ladies and gentlemen who may have come here in search of signed copies of the speaker's book that they are going to be bitterly disappointed, because his publishers have made a cock-up.' With forced jocularity he adds: 'I hope they weren't Colin Wilson's publishers, otherwise it's not surprising we can't find his books. Angus Wilson, I should say.'

Ignoring the interruption, Cody rises to address his diminishing audience, also in heavily jocular mode. 'But I'm sure you can find copies in Waterstone's, and if you'd like to form an orderly queue in the bar of the Metropole Hotel later, I'll be happy to sign them. Now are there any questions? That lady there.'

'What does the speaker think of Patrick Hamilton as a writer? Because.'

What the bloody hell is bloody Maureen doing here? 'Patrick who?'

Hamilton, you pillock. Piss-artist. *Rope. Gaslight. The West Pier. Hangover Square.* Vastly underrated writer, Duffy would tell anyone who cared to listen in the days when he could be bothered talking about books.

Now if Maureen's question had been directed at Duffy he would be away to the races. Having read just about everything Mister Hamilton ever wrote, going back to the time when he used to read anything at all. And coming to how he came to know Maureen: he happened to have just bought a second-hand copy of the reprint of *Twenty Thousand Streets Under the Sky* when he walked into the Whip Tavern one morning and got chatting to Maureen who was working behind the bar. Or rather, Maureen got chatting to him.

'I see you've got a book by that Patrick Hamilton. Did you ever know him or?'

'No, but I've always liked his stuff. Greatly underrated writer.'

But Maureen was not to be deflected into a literary symposium. 'Because we got to know him quite well, insofar as anybody. He used to come and stay with us when my mother ran a guest-house in Brunswick Crescent. I say used to. Did once, for five weeks, whilst he was writing his last book. But he wasn't a well man. Whether it was the drink.'

It is an oft-told tale and it is about to be told afresh to

Moss Cody who, little realising that he is about to jump into a well-baited trap, innocently continues:

'I know the name, of course, but I can't really claim to be familiar with his work. But did he write short stories, because that's what—'

'Short stories, long ones, who's counting, because he was a very very great writer. Shamefully neglected, would you agree, or?'

Cody flounders. '*West Pier* he wrote, I know that, so he would have been a Brighton writer, then?'

Duffy sees the opportunity to chip in and score. The writing scene he may not be as well up on as some people, but he does know his Patrick Hamilton.

'Not necessarily, my friend. You might just as well have said Earl's Court. West Ken. Hangover Square.'

'Although,' says Maureen.

'Wherever,' bluffs Cody.

'Because I knew him personally, don't you see,' Maureen ploughs on. 'He used to live with us when I was a girl back in. So.'

Oh, good Christ, don't let her get going on the Brunswick Crescent saga and the book Hamilton was writing, they will be here all bloody night. Duffy reasserts himself as interlocutor.

'It's getting beyond our time.' In fact they can't have done more than twenty minutes. 'Any last questions?'

The self-appointed chairman in the belted raincoat rises in the third row. 'I have a question, sir. Where do I go to get my money back?'

10

Evading the wrath of Moss Cody and the indignation of his audience, Duffy sneaks out of the Corn Exchange by a side door. But he does not escape Maureen, who has selected the same exit.

'Well, I must say that was a bit of a.' Let-down? Disappointment? Cock-up? Rip-off? Anticlimax? Maureen does not say. Possibly these uncompleted sentences do not resolve themselves even in her own mind. 'Because.'

'I know,' says Duffy wryly. 'Feel like a drink, Maureen? Because I certainly do!'

'Just a quick one, then I've.' Got to get back, it transpires. Shit. To pick up some notes she's made for the Writers' Workshop out at the Gardner Arts Centre. Yes. Duffy remembers a blue file on Maureen's hall table. He remembers it because that's where he left his Jiffy bag, on top of it.

The good news is that as yet she seemingly knows nothing of Duffy's unauthorised visit to her flat earlier. But how to get back there ahead of Maureen and scoop up the incriminating package?

He tries a desperate throw: 'Writers' Workshop, I thought it's been cancelled.'

'I don't think so, because.'

'I believe you'll find it has, Maureen. Team leader got laryngitis.'

'No, Chris, you're getting us mixed up with some other. I'd have heard.'

She would, too. Maureen attends every Writers' Workshop she can sniff out, in or out of the Festival season. Kind of thing she goes in for. Duffy once said she went to writers' workshops to stop herself from writing. Maureen was not best pleased. Said Duffy had some room to talk. In which, admittedly, she had a point.

All right, on to plan B. They are in the Pavilion Arms by now. Having got Maureen established at her usual table by the disused fireplace, he goes over to the bar and in a low voice orders two pints of Guinness, perfectly aware that she has asked specifically for a half.

'Oo, Chris, you've never got me a!'

'Do you good, Maureen.'

He takes a sip from his own glass, sets it down on the table and then histrionically smites his forehead.

'Bloody book!' And he puts before Maureen the glib explanation that he has left his signed copy of Moss Cody's opus behind at the Corn Exchange and must dash back for it before it is nicked. 'Shan't be a tick, Maureen. Don't drink my Guinness.'

'Chance would be a.'

On past performances it will take Maureen twelve minutes to get through a pint of Guinness. It should take Duffy five minutes to reach Sheridan Square, and five minutes back.

Duffy sets off at a sprint, losing a minute already as he gets tangled up with the Street Arts Showcase horizontal conga-line blocking the bottom of Queen's Road.

Hurries on to Sheridan Square. Lets himself in to Maureen's flat. Blue file still on her hall table, but no Jiffy bag containing Cody's book. All right, maybe that's not where he left it after all. Coffee table? Dining table? Bedside table? It's no longer on the premises. How odd.

It can't have fallen into Maureen's hands, she would have mentioned it. It's a mystery. Or perhaps, on reflection, not all that mysterious a mystery.

Duffy deals with the problem as he deals with all his problems: he goes for a drink.

The Pineapple, his local across the square, is nearest. By rights he should be making his way back to the Pavilion Arms where he left Maureen, but sod trekking up that hill. He can always spin her a yarn later: 'Sorry I missed you, Maureen. I got waylaid by one of those bloody writers in the Corn Exchange, the place is crawling with them. I hope you found a good home for my Guinness . . .'

He takes the risk of Olive being in the Pineapple: she isn't. Nor, thank Christ, is Eggo, who would still be trying to figure out how much commission he has lost on that bloody vase. Good. Duffy doesn't want any more confrontations, the Corn Exchange fiasco was all he needed for one day.

The Pineapple, a discreet front parlour of a pub like a doll's-house gin palace, used by regulars living in or around Sheridan Square and, like the best Brighton pubs, cautious with strangers, is, in the right circumstances, Duffy's favourite.

But these are not the right circumstances. Olive and Eggo may not be present but Mickey Daniels is. Bugger. He ought to be in the Crown and Two Chairmen at this hour.

It is too late to avoid Mickey and so Duffy has no option but to join him. Mickey, a pint at his elbow, is reading a book. An unusual activity for him. Duffy cannot make out the title but even if he could he wouldn't recognise it since he has blanked it out of his mind. But he does recognise the empty Jiffy bag at Mickey's feet.

'Never saw you as a big reader, Mickey.'

'No. And if they're all writing crap like this I never will be. Do you want it back?'

'How did you come by it in the first place?'

'Picked it up where you left it. Think I shouldn't have?'

Duffy answers with a shrug. Patently Mickey wants something of him. He will say what it is in his own good time.

'So what is it you're looking for in there, Duffy?'

'Who says I was looking for anything?'

'Well, we know you're giving Maureen one, but you don't have the run of the place.'

'No more do you, Mickey. So what were you after, this time round?'

'Maybe the same as you.'

Duffy would be very surprised. He's not even a hundred per cent sure he knows what he's looking for himself.

'And you found it, did you?'

'Might have done, might not.'

This is a game. Duffy is in no mood to play it. 'You've finished with my book, have you?' He reaches across for *Twelve Tales and Another*. Crap title, crap cover. Plug from one of the bearded buggers on the front cover. It could have saved Duffy's skin half an hour ago. As it is, he can still profit from it. Review copies fetch a third of the retail price at Discount Books, up by the station. Plus his modest appearance fee, the morning has not been entirely wasted.

'So you're not interested?' pushes Mickey.

If this were a round of poker, Duffy would raise Mickey and see him. He cannot have a strong hand. He does not know what Duffy is looking for. He does not know what he is looking for himself. As for having found it, pull the other one.

'What is it you might have that I could be remotely interested in?' asks Duffy, boldly languid.

Mickey smirkingly lights up, a lengthy performance that starts with his tapping the cigarette on the packet – an unnecessary ritual, since he is on filter-tips – and ends with his blowing smoke down his nostrils.

'Shall we say a certain old typescript, around three hundred pages?'

Jesus Christ, he knows, he's seen it, he's got it. The crafty bastard.

No reason why he shouldn't, if Duffy wants to be rational.

After all, she's told Duffy about it, no reason why she shouldn't have told Mickey about it too. Especially if, as Duffy has long suspected, he has been giving Maureen one on the sly.

One afternoon, with the sea-dappled sunlight stream-
ing in to her bedroom, Maureen had said with dreamy
pettishness – he had been saying something about getting
back to work, not that he'd been doing any, just that
as so often he was tiring of her company after the sex
bit was over – 'You writers, so-called, you're always
banging on about what you're. But you never.'

'What are you saying, Maureen?'

'Does it ever occur to you that I might've?'

'What? Written a book? You've never said.'

'You've never asked, have you? So.'

It emerged, the facts dragged out of her like pulled
teeth, that Maureen indeed claims to have written a
book. A novel. Set in Brighton. Hot stuff. What – porn?
No, but there were people still alive who might just.
Recognise themselves? Still alive from when? Oh, years
and years ago. And she'd never tried to get it published?
Good God, no, she wouldn't know where to.

'Have you never shown it to anyone?' asked Duffy.

'No, never.'

'I wouldn't mind reading it, one of these days.'

One of these days. Sound casual, for already he had
his suspicions.

But maybe too casual. 'One of these,' she'd echoed,
and changed the subject.

He has brought it up again, once or twice. 'You were
going to show me that book you wrote.'

'Was I? You'll have to wait until I can.'

Until she can do what? Find it? Be bothered? Duffy has
had one or two more tries at jogging the manuscript out
of her, but in the end he will have to find it himself.

Or, as it turns out, Mickey will. Or has already.

'And you've got it, have you?'

'No, but I know where it is,' says Mickey, unusually straightforward.

'Which is where?'

Mickey gives Duffy a pitying, wasn't-born-yesterday look and does not deign to reply.

'All right, you say it's an old typescript. How old?'

'Christ knows, but it wasn't done on a word processor, that's for sure. Manual typewriter, I'd say, and it's written in purple, so if that doesn't make it old I don't know what does.'

'And what kind of book is it, Mickey? I mean, is it a novel or an autobiography or what?'

'Fuck knows, mate. I've had trouble enough reading that shit you left behind in Maureen's gaff, let alone bundles of old purple typewriting.'

'Is there an author's name on it, that you recall?' Duffy asks this lightly, but with his heart in his mouth.

'Don't think so. Just the title.'

'Which is what?'

'Lemme see. *Palace Pier*.'

Duffy enjoys – endures – a frisson of excitement, an entirely physical one such as he imagines may be experienced by a cat having its chin tickled beyond endurance. He does not speak. He cannot speak.

Mickey says, all unconcerned: 'Why, something you've heard of?'

'No, never.'

And he hasn't. Maureen, curiously, has always refused to tell him the title. All she will say, when pressed, is:

'It hasn't got one yet – just a working title. So.' An expression she has picked up from one of her 'How to Write' manuals that occupy a foot of space between the bookends on her desk.

But working title or not, *Palace Pier* sounds promising. Duffy wouldn't make bets, but he would take bets. So where is the bloody manuscript?

Mickey isn't going to tell him.

'All right,' says Duffy, 'I won't ask you where it is, but how did you come to hear about it?'

'Olive.'

Olive?

'Olive? Jesus Christ, she's not got it stashed away in her room, has she?'

'She did have at one time but she put it back. Thought it might be valuable and she could be done for possession.'

'So where did you come across it, Mickey?'

'In Olive's room, of course.' Of course. Mickey regards himself as having the run of the house. Duffy would be surprised if the nosy sod hasn't given his own flat the once-over.

'And where did she put it back?'

'Where she found it. Don't try to catch me out, Duffy.'

'Sorry, Mickey, but you're losing me.'

Mickey knocks back his drink and looks meaningfully into his empty glass like the oldest-inhabitant narrator in the stories Duffy used to read in old bound volumes of the *Strand Magazine*. W. W. Jacobs. Christ, in those days you could live like a prince on 5,000 words a month.

Duffy gets them in. Mickey takes a long swig at his refill. This is clearly going to be a three-drink problem.

'Right. How much do you know about Maureen's mum?'

'Not a lot.'

'You know she kept a boarding-house in Brunswick Crescent?'

'Guest-house, yes. Theatrical digs.'

'Guest-house, theatrical digs and part-time knocking shop,' says Mickey, leaning back to savour the anticipated look of astonishment or incredulity on Duffy's face.

It is not forthcoming. For one thing, he never knew Maureen's mother, although he had heard rumours going way back. Rumours slosh around in Brighton like the tide washing against the pierheads. For another, like mother, like daughter. The contents of Maureen's wardrobe bottom drawer, the fur-lined handcuffs and suchlike items from the Boutique Bleu, had to have a history.

'And where does Olive come into it?'

'She used to work for Maureen's mum as a maid, so-called. Someone to let the punters in and turf them out. This was light-years ago, presumably before she went dotty.'

It is all slowly jigsawing together but still not forming a comprehensible enough picture for Duffy.

'So how does she come to be living in Maureen's attic in Sheridan Square?'

'Maureen gets married, her husband already owned the place, so she does no more, she moves out of

Brunswick Crescent and into Sheridan Square. From what I can gather, Olive just followed them, like a stray dog.'

'And sat up in the attic, collecting waste paper and going quietly mad. Why didn't they sling her out?'

Mickey taps his nose. 'I think she knows where too many bodies are buried.'

Very interesting, Duffy is sure, but more to the point is that she knows where that manuscript is buried.

And by what means has Mickey gleaned his information? By sitting quietly and patiently in a corner of the Pineapple listening to Olive chuntering away to herself about her grudges, past and present, against Maureen. Until she was barred.

'And you say Olive still knows where this manuscript is?' pursues Duffy, who is not interested in the case of Olive *v* Maureen.

'She does.'

'It all sounds a long time ago. How do we know it's still there?'

'We don't, but there's no reason to suppose it's been moved.'

'So how do we find out?' asks Duffy once again, not expecting a constructive answer. But this time Mickey is more encouraging.

'I would have thought there was a drink in this, Duffy.'

Duffy returns to the bar. Orders two large ones. Pours most of one of them in the other glass and tops his own up with soda.

'Cheers, Duffy.'

'All right, Mickey, when do I get to see it?'

Still playing him along, Mickey says waggishly: 'Ah, that's the question!' But it isn't, as it turns out. The question is, as he now formulates it: 'Depends what's in it for me.'

This poses a dilemma for Duffy. He cannot say what's in it for Mickey until he has seen the manuscript, and even then who knows? It's unquantifiable. If it's what he hopes it is, he will have to take expert advice. He cannot get expert advice until he has put a price on the manuscript. He cannot put a price on the manuscript until he has got expert advice.

'If we're talking about money—' he begins weakly.

'If we were talking about money, you'd be wasting my fucking time, because I know you haven't got any,' says Mickey with brutal candour. 'Now listen, Duffy, because I'm going to tell you what I'll do with you. I've got something you want that's no use to me, or at least I can put my hands on it, right? You've got something I want that's no use to you. Swap.'

What's he talking about? Oh, Christ, that. Completely forgotten about it.

'You mean that vase,' says Duffy as the penny drops.

'I mean that vase. Which by rights belongs to me in the first place.'

'Eggo should never have sold it to you, dozy prat that he is. Didn't he give you your money back?'

'No, he fucking didn't. Said he didn't have any cash on him.'

'I'll kill him,' says Duffy calmly. 'And when I've killed him I'll get the vase. See you in the Crown and Two in about an hour.'

11

Duffy reckons that somewhere in the back-streets of Brighton there is a school for bartenders which as well as showing its students how to mix a decent vodka martini or even, from the available evidence, not a very good one, teaches them how to juggle.

At any rate, every cocktail bar, jumped-up wine bar, sports bar or made-over pub or club seems to demand as a condition of employment that its bar staff know how to juggle with cocktail shakers, bottles, glasses, ice buckets, plates, ashtrays, peanut bowls or, in the case of the Bamboo Bar as Duffy crosses the threshold, a neatly-folded golf umbrella which the barman is balancing on his forehead.

There is no one else in the place. Duffy is not surprised. The barman shows no sign of acknowledging his presence, but with the peculiar crab-like splayed walk of the obsessive, if not accomplished, juggler, continues to stagger up and down behind the bar with the umbrella swaying precariously on his forehead.

Ultimately he has to reach up and grab it before it topples to the floor. 'Some you win,' says the barman ruefully, assuming, wrongly, that he has a captive audience in Duffy, who loathes juggling waiters even more than he loathes street theatre and human statues. 'On a good day I can tip it to the end of my nose, full three-hundred-and-sixty-degree swivel, then finish up with it balanced on my chin. The dimple helps. What can I do you for?' he asks, passing over a bar menu as he resumes the day job.

The prices. Sodding hell. They have gone up since yesterday, Duffy will swear it. Festival supplement, he supposes. Does he really want anything here? Yes, he does. Out of the corner of his eye he has caught sight of the vase. On a shelf behind the bar, now embellished by a bunch of paper pansies.

'I'll take a Bacardi Breezer, thanks,' says Duffy, with a horrified glance down the bar list. What the hell: in for a penny, in for £5.60. Out of Lizzie's twenty. It's to be hoped not only that Eggo takes some money on the stall, but that he doesn't pocket too much of it himself. 'And will you have one yourself?' asks Duffy ingratiatingly.

'Kind of you, I'll take a Snowball if that's all right with you.'

Yes, you just would, you juggling bastard, at seven quid a throw. As the barman tosses ingredients into his cocktail shaker and then predictably begins to run it up his sleeve and behind his back, Duffy decides to waste no time and get to the point before he's obliged to order another drink.

He clears his throat. 'Er – that vase up there?'

'Vase? Did you say vase?'

It is unfortunate that at this moment the cocktail shaker, which the barman has clasped between his shoulder-blades, slithers out of his control in the trickle of ice which is escaping from the shaker's loosened cap.

As a gunge of crushed ice, advocaat, fizzy lemonade and glacé cherries slowly covers the bar counter like a miniature avalanche, Duffy notes that the bastard was mixing his Snowball before Duffy's own Bacardi Breezer.

'Shit,' says the barman. 'Shall I do another one?'

'Please yourself,' shrugs Duffy. He doesn't realise, yet, that the juggling barman intends to charge him for them both.

He is anxious to get back to the agenda. 'That vase,' he says again.

'Yes, it's a nice vase, isn't it?' The barman adds archly: 'Ours is a nice vase ours is. It was left here for some reason, can't think why.'

'I know it was. I left it. Earlier today.'

'Very absent-minded of you.'

With a sinking heart Duffy realises that he is being sent up, or joshed with. He has a mortal distaste for joshing. If he had wanted to be joshed with, he would have emigrated to the United States.

'Listen, friend, I'm in a big hurry. Let me pay for the drinks, give me the vase, and I'll be on my way.'

'Give you the vase, did you say?'

'Give me the vase.'

'Why should I want to give you the vase?'

'Because it's my fucking vase!'

'Oh! Oh! Oh! Oh! Oh! Such language! How do we know it's your fucking vase? Got a receipt, have we?'

'No, I haven't got a receipt. Why should I want a receipt for my own property? Is the manager in?'

'I'm the manager.'

'Yes? You don't look like management material to me. Just give me the vase.'

The barman, or manager as he now affects to be, goes so far as to take the vase down off its shelf and remove its bouquet of paper flowers.

'This vase, would it be?'

'That vase,' says Duffy through gritted teeth, realising that he is going to have to humour the stupid bastard.

'Now you're sure it's this vase?'

'I'm sure it's that vase. Just hand it over, would you, and stop pissing about.'

'Language again,' says the barman mock-chidingly. 'I should have mentioned we have a little rule here, when it comes to cuss-words. Three strikes and you're out.'

'Look, give me the bill and give me the vase, and we'll say no more about it, all right?'

'Give you the vase, you say? *Give* you the vase?'

He is on the verge of saying, 'What's it worth?' The vase is on the bar counter. Duffy reaches over for it. The barman snatches it up. And begins juggling with it.

'Oh, Christ, please don't do that!' moans Duffy.

'Why? Valuable vase, is it? Pricey? Family heirloom, is it?'

The barman runs the vase up his right arm, tosses it to the left and runs it down his forearm. Clearly following a routine taught on the bartenders' school juggling course he tosses the vase over his shoulder, brings it down behind his back, recovers it, and begins the whole perilous rigmarole again.

Duffy dare not speak. If he did, it would be to point

out nervously that the barman is not a particularly accomplished juggler.

He finds voice as the barman goes into that portion of his act that earlier brought the golf umbrella in danger of crashing down about his ears.

'Don't *do* that!' says Duffy sharply.

Too late. With what seems to be slow-motion inevitability the vase rolls to the ground and quietly disintegrates on the tiled floor.

'Whoops-a-daisy!' titters the barman.

'You – stupid – prat.' It is a weary murmur rather than a cry of anguish, but it does not escape the barman's ears.

'That's it. We don't do language here, sir. Pay up and leave.'

'Pay up? Pay up?' screeches Duffy. 'You've just smashed a very valuable vase!'

'Valuable my arse,' says the barman. 'There's your bill. If you don't pay it before you go, and I know who you are, I'll see you barred from every pub from Kemp Town to Hove.'

Duffy knows when he is up against the Brighton mafia. *Brighton Rock* isn't in it. He draws the bill towards him.

'Jesus Christ! Wait a minute – you've charged me for two of those sodding Snowballs.'

'Yes, sir. If you remember, I very unfortunately spilled the first so then you ever so kindly bought me another one. Cheers.'

12

The Crown and Two Chairmen is an extension of the
North Laine street markets. A typical pocket handker-
chief pub, it is occupied entirely by dealers and street
traders muttering to one another and passing over wads
of grubby banknotes. Mickey is not yet there – not
that it matters now whether he turns up or not – but
Eggo is, in, for some reason, a state of suppressed
excitement.

A natural sidler, a human crab who never walks when
he can scuttle, Eggo edges up to Duffy as he orders
himself a bottle of beer.

'I won't have a drink, boss, not just now.'

'Too bloody true you won't, Eggo. Who's looking
after the stall?'

'Mater mine. I said you'd see him all right.'

'Piss off. Has Mickey Daniels been in?'

'That mater yours? He's looking for you, enny?
Gimme a right mouthful, he did, over that vaise. He
cops on that legalistically speaking, it's his property,
know what I mean?'

'Legalistically, Eggo, he's probably right. Unless you
gave him his money back, as I told you to.'

'What, his ten quid, boss?'

'His eight quid, Eggo.'

'I shudder said eight quid. I din have it by me. He says he's gunna have a word with you about it.'

'Nothing to do with me, Eggo. You'd just better give him his money.'

'Else his vaise,' says Eggo, with a crafty wink.

'His vase, for your information, when last seen was lying in two thousand pieces on the floor of the Bamboo Bar.'

To Duffy's surprise Eggo opens his all but toothless mouth, throws back his head and emits what sounds like a bronchial death-rattle which, although he has never heard Eggo laugh below, he correctly identifies as an approximation of mirth.

'That's all right, boss. My oh my,' wheezes Eggo. 'Oh dearie me. Now you just drink up and foller me, and I betcher I'll have us both off the hook before we're finished.'

'I wasn't aware of being on the hook in the first place,' says Duffy testily, but not entirely truthfully. 'But what's this all about?'

'Trust in me, boss.'

Clearly Eggo has got something up his sleeve. While not over-blessed with intelligence, he does have a certain cunning, and he does know his way around this end of Brighton. Whatever he is on to, there will be something in it for Eggo. But by the sound of it, there could be something in it for Duffy too.

Duffy does not exactly follow Eggo as requested, for Eggo is not a natural leader of men. He suffers Eggo to trot eagerly at his side, servilely directing him around the occasional street corner. Duffy has never bothered to look up in his reading of old-fashioned fiction what type of breed a whipped cur might be, but if Eggo were a dog he would be in the whipped-cur class.

Presently they reach a down-at-heel street near the station where what were once small shops and workshops are now dealers' lockups and storerooms. Eggo, almost panting with anticipatory delight, brings Duffy to a stop outside a narrow, open-fronted little warehouse with its interior piled high with cardboard crates.

Parked on the pavement is an anonymous white van whose particulars a traffic warden is woodenly jotting down, while two men in khaki dust-coats scurry in and out of the warehouse unloading the cardboard crates. These are stamped: THIS SIDE UP. FRAGILE. BURSLEY CERAMICS. Automatically, Duffy is transported to Mister Bennett's Five Towns. What a stroke of luck that must have been, to be brought up with your own material all around you. Like being Van Gogh and born in a field of sunflowers.

He recalls himself to humdrum Brighton. 'So what's going on here, Eggo?'

Eggo taps his nose and beckons Duffy into the inner recesses of the warehouse. He is evidently known to the management, for no one raises any objection when he rips the masking tape off one of the packing cases and, plunging his hand into a clutter of protective tissue paper, brings up an exact replica of the vase Duffy has just relinquished in smithereeens on the floor of the Bamboo Bar.

'And they've got six hundred of the bleeders!' cackles Eggo.

So Duffy, insofar as he has thought about it at all, was right in the first place. Doubtless destined for the amusement arcades and souvenir stands along the front. With any luck, Mickey will never see them. He never goes along the front, he hates the sea.

'Transfer-printed lustreware,' says a voice behind him, that of one of the men who was bringing in the packing cases, obviously the boss. 'They're very much coming back into vogue. Usually bought in pairs.'

'Yes, I know,' says Duffy, turning the vase in his hands as if he knows something about the subject. 'What are you asking for them?'

'Are you in the trade?'

'He's my boss,' says Eggo proudly. Duffy's fellow-boss does not look as if he regards this as much of a recommendation.

'How many did you want?'

'One.'

'One case?'

'One vase.'

Even Eggo recognises this for the *faux pas* it is. 'Thing is, boss, it's wholesale.'

'Minimum one case,' says the boss dismissively, and turns away, as if to attend to better things. Eggo takes a step forward to interpose himself between the boss and Duffy, and in doing so, seems symbolically to come into his own.

'What's your best on this, Oliver?'

'To you, Eggo? Twelve for nine, and I'm robbing myself.'

This is gibberish to Duffy, but piecing together the

ensuing bargaining, he gathers that he is being offered a dozen vases for the price of nine, this being adjusted by Eggo's haggling to eight.

It strikes Duffy that Eggo is turning out to be far better at his job than he, Duffy, is at his own, whatever he reckons that to be.

There then comes the delicate matter of payment. After shelling out for exotic drinks at the Bamboo Bar from the twenty pounds lent to him by Lizzie, Duffy does not find himself greatly in funds.

Again Eggo takes charge. He doesn't have any money either, but he enters into a series of overlapping negotiations with the warehouse boss, whereby before the evening is out he will be repaying monies that are owing to A, having collected them from B who owes them to him, whereupon A will return to C funds that are due to Duffy.

Duffy knows nothing of these subterranean transactions and doesn't want to know. Eggo is smarter than he ever realised. Or perhaps smarter is not the word. Call it craftier. It is enough for him that upon spitting on his palm and shaking hands with Eggo – a ritual which goes back to long before Duffy's days on the Golden Mile, probably to the gypsies who were its first inhabitants – the wholesaler thrusts a cardboard case of lustreware vases into his arms.

He owes Eggo a large one. He takes him into the little pub around the corner – there is a little pub around every corner in this neighbourhood, and indeed in almost every neighbourhood in Brighton. He sets the cardboard packing case down on a table, brings over a large Scotch, a beer for himself, and sits down, facing Eggo in what he hopes is recognisably a serious manner.

Having almost ceremoniously opened the case and extracted one vase and examined it for blemishes, he puts it down carefully on the floor between his feet and says: 'Now, Eggo. We've got eleven of these vases here.'

'Yes, boss. I'll be sure not to put them all out at once,' says Eggo cunningly, repeating the knowing nose-tapping business.

Duffy lowers his voice.

'You won't put them out at all, Eggo. What you'll do, you'll take them down to the beach after dark and drop them into the sea.'

Eggo is genuinely shocked.

'Chuck them in the sea?' He puzzles, then gives a good impression of light dawning. 'Oh, I get it, boss. You've had the one today, avenchew? The extra drop. The odd gargle.'

'Just do as you're told, Eggo.'

'But they'd float, boss.'

'Fill them with pebbles, you berk!'

'But boss, think how much we could make by putting 'em on the stall and flogging 'em!'

'We?'

'You.'

'Eggo. Listen. For reasons I'm not going to go into, I don't want Mickey Daniels to know there's more than one of these vases.'

'But he knows already, boss.'

Duffy's inflated estimation of Eggo's intellect sinks

back to its former level. He experiences the all-too-familiar feeling when he is around Eggo: that he is in the presence of unreconstructed hopelessness.

'For God's sake, Eggo – you mean you've told him?'

'I had to, boss. He kept banging on about his ten quid.'

Duffy has had more constructive conversations with street bollards. He finishes his beer and rises wearily.

'So what have I to do with these vaises, boss?'

'Stick 'em up your jacksey.'

As Duffy returns to the Crown and Two Chairmen, Mickey Daniels is propping up the bar counter, talking to a street trader in the furtive, side-of-the-mouth manner which characterises certain Brighton dealers. Without greeting Duffy, Mickey brusquely removes the vase from his arms and places it with exaggerated reverence into the hands of the street trader.

'Sample,' says Mickey. Somehow, the brisk transfer of the vase relegates Duffy to the role of his assistant or runner, an Eggo.

The trader holds the vase up to the light and makes a performance of scrutinising it carefully, turning it around the full 360 degrees.

'Bursley Ceramics,' says the trader. 'Repro.'

'If you say so,' says Mickey. It gives Duffy irrelevant pleasure to reflect that after all Mickey knows as much or as little about pottery as he does himself.

'And you say you can do me five dozen?' says the trader.

'I can do you ten dozen if you like,' says Mickey carelessly.

'Five'll do for the time being, Mickey – don't want to flood the market. All right, you're on.'

Extending a palm, he repeats the spitting ritual which earlier sealed the contract between Eggo and the wholesaler. Duffy feels an outsider in these transactions. That, one half of his psyche tells him, is as it should be. The writer is an outsider, an observer, the kid peering longingly through the sweetshop window. But his other half pines to be in the sweetshop. Yet he can never remember having been in it. Even in Blackpool, his homeland, when working on the dodgems, he always felt he was giving the impression of someone who was only playing at working the dodgems.

Momentarily, surrounded by all this market-stall camaraderie, he is consumed with self-pity. A trait he could put to profitable professional use if only he knew what to do with it.

Mickey and the street trader have withdrawn into a huddle at the end of the bar, where Duffy sees a wad of notes changing hands. In Mickey's favour. There should be a drink in this.

The trader departs, clutching his sample vase. Mickey, with a self-satisfied Peter Lorre smirk, returns to join Duffy.

'So that seems to have worked out well in the end,' ventures Duffy.

'For some,' says Mickey.

'Worth a jar, I would have thought.'

'Bollocks. I didn't get where I am today buying drinks for prats like you.' Nevertheless, Mickey, in jovial mode, peels off a twenty-pound note and calls for large ones.

Having clinked glasses, and feeling more like Eggo than ever, Duffy says diffidently: 'So now we come to your part of the bargain.'

'What fucking bargain?' scoffs Mickey.

'I was going to get you the vase – which I did.'

'After a fashion. I had a cross-eyed retriever once that was better at fetching rabbits than you are at fetching vases.'

'– and you were going to get me that manuscript . . .'

'I haven't got your fucking manuscript.'

'– tell me where it is, I should have said,' amends Duffy.

'You should, mate. I've already told you where it is, if you'd only cleaned your ears out and listened.'

Has he? Perhaps he has. Duffy remembers him rambling on about Olive finding the thing but none of the details stay with him. Memory loss. It's getting worse.

'It's back in that house in Brunswick Crescent that Maureen's mum used to own.'

Chilton Court. They're big, those houses in Brunswick Crescent. 'Whereabouts, Mickey?'

'How the fuck do I know? It's in a trunk with some other gear the geezer what owned it left. He was always gunna come back for it, but he never did, did he?'

'So where's this trunk, Mickey?'

'Wherever you put trunks. Cellar, I think – Christ knows. It's your problem, mate, not mine.'

It is indeed. Duffy can just see himself rolling up to Chilton Court: 'Oh, Mrs Cooney, good morning, I wonder if I might go down to your cellar and rummage around in an old trunk that was left here some years ago . . .' Fat chance.

He could always break in, of course, but knowing his luck and his lack of burglarising expertise, that would finish up a police job. Or, now here was an idea, he could even book himself a room for a couple of nights at Chilton Court. Whereupon Mrs Cooney would be straight on the blower to her pal Maureen, asking what his game is when he's already got a perfectly good home to go to.

It will have to be thought about, when next he is in a mood to do some thinking.

Meanwhile he has the serious problem of having just about run out of cash. No use asking Mickey to spare a twenty off that fat roll of banknotes: Mickey is one of life's borrowers rather than a lender.

Duffy waits for Mickey to finish his drink in the slim hope that there will be another one forthcoming, but Mickey pushes aside his drained glass with the air of someone who, if he is going to have another, isn't going to be the one who pays for it.

He will have to hope Eggo takes some money on the stall this afternoon, otherwise he will just have to get a sub from Maureen. Again. Not even counting today's rent, he already owes her enough to pay off the National Debt. Where is all this going to end? Apart from off the end of the pier?

Until Eggo packs up the stall for the day, he has the afternoon to waste. Or, to be more constructive, he has a free afternoon.

He seriously considers going home to write. Now

there would be a novel experience. Get out the old portable, stack of typing paper if he's still got any – he uses a lot up on his letters to the *Guardian* – and start writing. Not *Blackpool Rock*, that's going nowhere. So what to write? First lesson from all the correspondence schools: write about what you know. But what does he know? Fuck-all.

Brighton. There's a subject. Day in the life of, that kind of thing. With himself as hero, or anti-hero. Street trader, layabout, pubaholic. Bit like the Brighton end of that autobiography he's been planning, but true. How can he go wrong?

He'll marshal his thoughts and start writing straight away. As soon as he's cleaned his tennis shoes. No, first thing in the morning. Not now – tomorrow. Fresh. Tomorrow's another day.

But then it always was, wasn't it?

13

He has to programme the rest of the day. Go for a bit of a wander, scrape his loose change together and see if it will run to a last, drawn-out beer, give Eggo chance to rake in whatever takings the day might bring, shake the bugger upside down and pocket the dibs.

Leaving Mickey to his own devices in the pub he sets off on his bit of a wander, up the steep little streets towards the station, hoping for a pub doorway where he might spot a friendly face. Trouble is, none of the friendly faces he knows in Brighton ever has any money. They think, on the contrary, that Duffy does. Maybe he has talked too much in the past about the success of his book. Some people think all writers are millionaires. Not being one, Duffy has difficulty in admitting that he isn't.

He wanders onwards and upwards in zig-zag fashion until he finds himself, at last, above the Festival tree-line and out of tambourine-rattling reach of the hordes of street harpists, flautists, violinists, cellists, banjo players, bongo drummers, mime artistes, puppeteers, body-paint workshops, Irish line dancers, hip-hop dancers and the familiar chorus of unicyclists, stilt-walkers, clowns and jugglers, all of them desperately performing to the hilt as if on the orders of some mad film director concocting an ambitious epic in which they will play the street people.

He has by now reached a familiar shabby thorough-fare behind the station. Familiar, because going right back to the time he first came down to Brighton, there's a second-hand bookshop he used to haunt, almost the replica of one he used to haunt in Blackpool. Every town had at least one, then: now many of them are haunted only by the ghosts of authors long dead or out of print. Mister Maugham, Mister Priestley, Mister Galsworthy, Mister Hardy, Mister Chesterton.

It was never one of what is now the general run of second-hand bookshops, stocked with publishers' remainders, cheap reprints and paperbacks, but a proper second-hand bookshop such as Duffy remembered from his youth, like that guy in Mister Orwell's *1984*. Mister Kersh, Mister Saroyan, Mister Waugh. The shelves crammed tight with bulky hardbacks, and the dusty floor piled with the overflow.

He used to buy a clutch of books there every Saturday. Later, he used to sell a clutch of books there every Monday. Now he thinks of all the writers he has traded in and out of the place, as if it were a literary pawnshop. Mister Lawrence. Mister Thurber. Mizz Woolf. Mizz Murdoch. Mister Ackroyd.

It's a long time now since he last visited the dark little shop. A long time now since he read anything that didn't appear on newsprint. Why is that? Habit. It's like eating your daily intake of bran flakes. Eat your Faulkner. Drink up your Mailer.

He never learned the name of the little guy who ran the

shop, but he would always have a word. Always knew something about the books Duffy bought, or, later, sold. He'd even heard of *Razzle-Dazzle*. Said that a couple of years ago someone had come in looking for a copy but he didn't have one. Offered to put a search out, but the man had said not to bother, he was from Croydon and he didn't get into Brighton all that often.

This is the place. Same little shop, blistering red paintwork, could do with a makeover, God forbid such a thing ever happening. Or is it? No, this is blistering green paintwork, and bilious with it.

Something wrong here. There used to be first editions in that little shop window. Bargains, some of them – Mister Joyce Carey, if you were into Mister Carey; Mister Wodehouse, Mister Barstow. *Enemies of Promise*, which Duffy has never read although he knows what's in it, because he daren't read it.

They were in neat little pyramids. In their place is now a revolving orange light, such as you might find in a mobile-phone shop or something of the kind, or on the roof of a police car. Such as you do find, in fact, since something of the kind is what it has become. The Bookmine, it was called. Now it's Vid Viewing. In place of Mister Carey and Co. there is a clutch of raunchy-looking DVDs. Enemies of promise.

If Duffy had half a brick he would know how to put it to good use. He peers through the screen of multicoloured plastic strips that now masks the open doorway, giving it the appearance of a Soho porn shop. Blaring music within. Two sharp, shirt-sleeved young men lollingly in charge. No sign of the old boy who knows all about books – probably dead, or in the hospital with something terminal. That would be suitably Orwellian.

Duffy retreats glumly, to run the gauntlet of Festival roistering until he reaches the stall, where he finds Eggo packing up and lowering the tarpaulin. Eggo has had a good day, having sold not only a fair amount of bric-à-brac but his entire stock of lustreware vases. Mickey Daniels will kill him for encroaching upon his lucrative market, but it will do Eggo no harm at all to be killed. Duffy pays him off, trousers the cash and repairs to the Cricketers'. How to pass Saturday evening.

14

Saturday, though, is not his favourite night of the week. It is infested, from Duffy's observation, by the vocal equivalent of party noisemakers, an unfocused rowdiness made up of coarse laughing, as distinct from laughter, and loud voices doing their best to outshout each other. No point in moving on, though; the whole of Brighton is heaving at this hour. He would never come out on Saturday night, except for the fear that he would be missing something by staying in.

There is no one he knows in the crowded Cricketers' – young people, popcorn-clutching cinema-goers of the worst sort on the way to or from a film they have been told to see by *What's New, What's Naff in Brighton, Hove & Shoreham-by-Sea*; clubbers on the way to their grotty clubs, pubbers on their way to the next pub.

To save himself further hassle at the bar Duffy buys a bottle of wine and fights his way through to a corner perch he has just seen vacated, whether temporarily or not he neither knows nor cares – probably not, since the previous occupant of six precious inches of banquette has left behind a good three-quarters of a pint. Fuck him.

'Excuse me, I think this place is taken,' says a middle-aged woman as he squeezes in.

'Was,' says Duffy. He's in that kind of mood. That bastard manuscript. He got the worst of the bargain there, all right. There must be some way of getting his fists on it.

He could hire someone, bribe someone, to book a room at Chilton Court. Give him instructions where to find the trunk, insofar as he knows himself. Tell him what he's looking for. Instruct him to bring it back with no questions asked, like a golden retriever.

Preferably someone he's never met before. Why? Because that's how it happens in *Strangers on a Train*. But wait a minute. In Mister Chandler's screenplay, it's a swap arrangement – the proposal is that the pair, whatever their names were, should exchange murders. So if Duffy infiltrates someone into Chilton Court, what does he have to do in return? Not a murder, he hopes and trusts.

Is Duffy entirely sober? Perhaps not.

The man whose place he has appropriated returns from the Gents'. Burly bugger.

'Sorry, have I taken your seat?' asks Duffy placatingly.

'Fret not, mate, stay where y'are.'

The burly one picks up his pint glass and, clutching it like a grizzly bear carrying home a treat of bamboo shoots for its cubs, shambles out into the cobbled coachyard, as it used to be, adjoining the bar.

'I don't suppose you feel like spending a night at the Chilton Court private hotel? Including breakfast?'

Perhaps a no. Pacific though the bear may be, that would be just asking for a smack in the mouth. Which, in his present simmering frame of mind, Duffy is almost certain to get in any case before this night is over.

So if not *Strangers on a Train*, what? Duffy runs his fertile mind through a wide selection of alternatives. False moustaches. Fake gas inspectors. Hiring a private detective – now there's a thought: Brighton, of all places, cannot be short of private detectives. But the reputable ones would draw the line at burglary and the disreputable ones would leave him open to blackmail. Think again.

He has got as far as renting the basement next door to Chilton Court and drilling through the cellar walls when he sees that his bottle of wine is finished already. Christ, that was quick. Ah, but he will have the world to know it was only 75 centilitres, according to the label. Duffy, when he takes it by the bottle, is used to litres.

He is just draining his glass and wondering whether to invest in another of the small, practically miniature, 75 cc bottles, when inspiration strikes. That agent he's signed up with, what's his bloody name again? Him. Gregory Thing. He would be only too glad of a free night's board at Chilton Court, and who better to recover the manuscript – what does he think he is getting his commission for?

So what is a manuscript penned by his client Chris Duffy – or so it is to be presumed, since his client has yet to set eyes on it – what is it doing in a trunk in the cellar of a private hotel in Brunswick Crescent?

Easy. Duffy owes Maureen Christ knows how much in back rent, and way back she confiscated the script of his novel *Palace Pier* till he paid up, depositing it at Chilton

Court where it remains in the custody of her friend Mrs
Cooney. So unless Gregory Thing has twenty-six weeks'
rent about his person . . .

That should do it. He will buff the story up a bit on
the way to the Festival Club, which should be opening
around now. With any luck this Gregory, Coates, that's
the name, should be there, bumming free drinks.

He isn't. Bugger has gone to the pictures, Duffy
reckons. He is just the kind of prat who goes to the
cinema Saturday nights.

Moss Cody, though, has not gone to the pictures. If
he had, it would be some bloody art film. Something
foreign, it was to be imagined. *The Wages of Fear* is
the last foreign film Duffy recollects seeing half of. He
expects others will have been made since.

Moss Cody, wandering moodily around the Festival
Club, looks as if he is spoiling for a fight. That's all
right by Duffy: so is he. They have yet to clear the air
over the fiasco of their Corn Exchange interview earlier
in the day. Duffy blames Cody for that: the prat has no
idea how to go about being interviewed. But doubtless
Cody will blame Duffy.

Duffy argues better with a glass in his hand. He thrusts
his way through the scrum surrounding the bar and
acquires two glasses of Chardonnay. The second one
is for later.

Turning to manoeuvre his way out of the throng,
he almost bumps into a young woman who is chatting to, or chatting up, a bearded young bugger bearing a plastic name-badge on what should by rights
be a blue velvet smoking jacket, but which on this

occasion is an oatmeal roll-neck sweater that looks as if it were formerly the property of Mister Colin Wilson.

She, however, is wearing a fetching bottle-green corduroy jacket that could have come out of the bearded bugger's wardrobe and probably did, for all Duffy knows. She is the kind of girl men lend their jackets to on cold evenings and but for a fatal flaw would be eminently fanciable. Duffy hates her on sight, or rather on sound, on account of her but-surely, hectoring, I'm-better-read-than-you, *Guardian*-subscribing, BBC *Woman's Hour* voice.

'But surely,' she is wittering to the bearded bugger, 'Firbank isn't still read in this day and age?'

Mister Firbank to you, you ignorant cow. And what do you mean by 'this day and age'? You don't throw writers off like last season's kitten heels, you know.

Aloud Duffy says: 'Wrote his stuff on blue postcards. Pioneered Mister Waugh.'

There's an unprinted rule at the Festival Club that one is welcome to join in any conversation going. The bearded bugger seems unaware of it. Ignoring Duffy he says to the *Woman's Hour*-sounding young lady:

'That's what I've been telling them. But the silly stubborn BFs want the Firbank piece before they'll let me do my Anthony Burgess.'

Here's an opportunity for Duffy. 'I used to know Mister Burgess,' he volunteers with some pride. 'Never forget sitting up all night with him at the Ilkley Festival when we demolished an entire bottle of brandy. God, could that man talk!'

He has not so much lost his audience as never found it. Bearded bugger talks over him:

'So you see, I'm between a rock and a hard place.'

Woman's Hour makes sympathetic clucking noises and then asks: 'Where's that from – I've often wondered?'

'What's that?' asks bearded bugger.

'Rock and hard place. Who said it?'

'Biblical,' chips in Duffy, without the faintest idea whether it is or not.

Bearded bugger, suspecting as much, asks keenly: 'Which book?'

'*Oxford Dictionary of Quotations*,' quips Duffy, for Woman's Hour's amusement. She smiles, gratifyingly. Perhaps not too *Woman's Hour* after all.

But Duffy's reputation as a wit is open to challenge.

'Don't talk to this clown about books,' slurs an aggressive voice at Duffy's elbow. 'I doubt if he's ever read a book in his life.'

Swaying, and clutching a tumbler of what looks like neat whisky, Moss Cody has apparently been seeking Dutch courage before any confrontation with Duffy. Duffy now has the option of thumping him or verbally crushing him. He makes what initially seems to be the right choice but which will prove to have been the wrong one.

'Some books you don't even need to read,' Duffy ripostes, or imagines that he is riposting.

Moss Cody addresses the bearded bugger, Woman's Hour and anyone else who cares to listen: 'This prick was supposed to be interviewing me about my new short-story collection this morning. He'd never set eyes on it, much less read it.'

'You can judge a book by its cover,' returns Duffy.

'You never even saw the cover, man! How can you judge a book when you haven't even read the blurb? Have you?'

'No, but I've read the bloody awful title.'

'You can't judge a book by its title either,' is the best Moss Cody can manage.

Duffy is warming up nicely. 'Listen, sunshine. I've judged books I've only ever seen wrapped up in parcels of twenty on the floor of Waterstone's.'

Duffy glances covertly towards Woman's Hour. She's enjoying this: will recount it later to some starling-chattering gathering of her bookish friends in the Groucho Club or wherever: 'Goodness, I thought at one stage they were about to come to blows.' She hasn't heard the half of it yet. Nor has the bearded bugger, who is obviously hugging himself and storing up an anecdote like a squirrel hoarding nuts.

Moss Cody has the floor. 'And your qualifications are what? You call yourself a writer, do you?'

'Yes. Do you?' The question Mister Bennett's Card would have asked, if Master Cody had ever heard of him.

'I do make a reasonable living as a professional writer, yes.'

It is as if Moss Cody has chalked a bull's-eye target on the seat of his jeans and bent over to be kicked.

Duffy's foot tingles. He can take his time over this. The row is building up quite an audience by now.

The splay-footed Pol Crosby waddles across to join the company. Good. Valuable witness. She will spread the word.

Duffy's response is not new. It is not even his own. It is one he has used before, effectively. If he were able to acknowledge the authorship he would, for Duffy, who would cheerfully purloin an entire manuscript without attribution, and indeed is hopeful shortly to be doing so, is scrupulous in giving chapter and verse on a sentence-by-sentence basis.

'You a professional writer?' says Duffy, measuring his words and raising his voice. 'Listen. You couldn't write fuck in the dust on a venetian blind.'

He is playing to a gallery whose front row contains Woman's Hour, the bearded bugger, Pol Crosby and a straggle of drinkers who have drawn up to watch the fun.

What Duffy, gratified at having elicited a full-throated chuckle from Woman's Hour and even a snigger from the bearded bugger, has not realised is that Moss Cody is playing to the gallery also. Luckily for Duffy, his aim is a bad one. He lunges out with his right fist and succeeds only in landing a blow on Duffy's left shoulder.

Duffy, clutching a full glass of wine in either hand, is not seriously hurt, but he is seriously taken off balance. He staggers backwards across the bar, which, as it comes crashing to the floor with its paraphernalia of glasses and bottles, reveals itself to be a mere pair of trestle tables covered by white cloths. Duffy, having the bad luck to sink between the two, collapses to the ground, taking the tables with him, jack-knifing around his ears. It is fortunate for him, or perhaps not so fortunate, that there is no press photographer on hand. 'Writers in Festival Fracas' would have been a good headline.

But all is not lost. Despite his humiliation, as Moss Cody is removed by security men and he is helped to his feet by a tut-tutting Pol Crosby who can scarcely disguise her glee at a literary row to jolly up a literary festival, Duffy feels reasonably pleased with himself. He permits himself an inward smile, which expands into a posed, rueful grin as a young man with a spiral notebook hurries across.

'Could I have a word, sir? I'm with the *Worthing Herald* . . .'

Fame at last.

SUNDAY

15

Sunday lunchtime usually finds Duffy in the Colonnade
Bar fronting the Brighton Theatre Royal. It was early
Edwardian when he first knew it; since then it's had a
makeover and is now late Victorian. But it still looks
the part. It's the kind of pub that every regional theatre
used to have and some still do, plastered with ancient
playbills and framed photographs, lavishly inscribed,
of the stars and nearly-stars who've performed next
door. Cosy.

But it's not so much the decor as the company that
appeals to Duffy. Sunday is when the coming week's
production 'gets in', as the theatrical expression has it,
last week's show having 'got out' on the previous night
straight after the second performance.

The Colonnade Bar at these times is much used by
stage crews, company managers and assistant stage managers in their break from their labours under the harsh
working light of the bare Theatre Royal stage. Occasion-
ally, on these Sundays, an actor will appear, usually an
ingénue, down from London or wherever was the most
recent date of the tour, and anxious not to be late for
tomorrow's rehearsal.

Duffy likes to chat to these theatricals and buy them
drinks, which, unlike some of the writers at present

infesting the Festival, they are always careful to reciprocate. Although he never attends a performance under any circumstance, Duffy takes to the theatre. He has always had it in mind to write a play if only he can think of one. The idea of dress rehearsals, production conferences, try-outs in the provinces, and shagging the leading lady, has always appealed. Not to mention the income: his mouth waters when he thinks of what Mister Hamilton is supposed to have made out of *Rope* and *Gaslight*. He supposes this attraction was an element of his brief marriage to Mags, back up there in Blackpool. He did start a play, a staged version of *Razzle-Dazzle*, but he went out of his depth and it is like so many unfinished projects in a drawer or a suitcase somewhere.

As so often when his first port of call is at opening-time, Duffy is early. He finds himself hanging about in New Road outside the Theatre Royal, stroking a bruised cheek from last night's little fracas and waiting for the Colonnade Bar to open. Idly, he watches a bill-poster stripping off last week's posters from the wall hard by the theatre foyer – yet another Alan Ayckbourn, lucky bugger – and putting up the replacements advertising the production starting tomorrow.

Next week's production features Nigel Spruce and Richard Wolesey, two tolerably well-known television actors, in a touring revival of a mid-Sixties boulevard comedy called *Say Who You Are*, together with one Alison Fairburn whom Duffy has never heard of, but who must enjoy a modicum of fame since her name is in the same-size type as the two men.

Duffy watches as the bill-poster pastes up the adjoining

sheet. It reads, together with the names of the director and set designer, 'With Mags Dodd'. Such is Duffy's alcoholic Alzheimer's that he does not at once recognise his former wife's name.

A cultured woman's voice behind him murmurs: 'I told you I'd become a *with*, didn't I?'

It was their first shared joke, when they'd picked one another up in Blackpool's equivalent of the Colonnade Bar, near the Grand Theatre. 'I may never be top of the bill,' she'd said, 'but if the right parts come along it shouldn't be too long before I'm a *with* under the title. Either that or an *and*.'

'Just so long as you're not a *but*,' Duffy had quipped. She was amused, and they had slept together that same night – an act of which he has but the haziest recollection.

She has worn well. Maturity suits her. How old must she be by now? Fiftyish? Getting on sixty? She doesn't look it.

'How are you, Chris?' says Mags, giving him a peck. 'More to the point, how am I?'

'You're looking terrific,' says Duffy truthfully. 'But your voice has got posher.'

'I get posher parts.'

Like her three co-stars Mags is something of a television name by now. People stare at her as they pass by, inducing in Duffy a proprietorial frisson of pleasure. But for himself, he never watches the box.

The Colonnade Bar has by now opened its doors, and by unspoken mutual consent they drift inside. 'Still first in, last out, I see,' says Mags.

'What are you having – whisky and Coke?' He remembers her drink. His marriage is coming back to him.

'Not when I'm working – I'll have a spritzer.'

'But you're not working today, Sunday?'

'It's our first date of the tour, so we have a tech this evening.' Tech – he recalls the expression. The technical rehearsal when they run through the lighting, changes of costume and suchlike. He remembers whiling away bored evenings in strange pubs while Mags, for hour upon hour, waited to rehearse her brief entrance as a parlourmaid. He would have a whisky and Coke lined up for her and then they would go back to the digs and jump into bed. He is beginning to feel quite nostalgic for those far-off days and to wonder why they got divorced. If they ever did. Did they?

After three or four Duffy is emboldened to blurt out: 'Can I ask you a personal question, Mags? Are we still divorced?'

Mags giggles. 'We never got round to getting a divorce. Why – do you want one?'

Duffy is puzzled. 'Not particularly. But if we're still married, what was all that legal-looking bumph that came by registered post years ago?'

'Didn't you read it?'

'No, I didn't see the point. Anyway, I don't like official stuff full of wherebys and heretofores. I put it away somewhere.'

'Same old Chris. If you'd bothered to read it, you would have seen it's nothing to do with divorce, except in a halfway house sort of way. It's a court maintenance order.'

He is even more puzzled. 'But I've never paid you maintenance.'

A bitter little laugh from Mags. 'Don't we know it! The solicitor told me I should have taken out an arrears summons but I was earning good money in a telly series at the time so I didn't bother. As I said to him, if I wanted a hobby, I'd take up trying to get blood out of stones.'

'Then why did you bother to take out this maintenance order?'

'You struck gold with that first novel of yours, Chris. I reckoned if you ever produced a second I should be entitled to half the takings.'

Can she do that? The question is so far academic.

Mags goes on, a taunting note he remembers of old creeping into her voice. Yes: that was why they got divorced. Or failed to get divorced, as it turns out. 'But there won't be a second, will there, Chris, or we'd have seen it by now. In that wonderful world of letters you used to dabble in, you're not even an *and* or a *with*, are you? To quote your own joke back at you, you're a *but*.'

At least she remembers his one good line. But Duffy, stung, tries to sound as if he has an as yet untapped store of secret resources. 'You never know, Mags, you never know. Come on, I'll take you to lunch.'

Why he should be doing such a thing he would be hard put to say. Could be he is grateful that she has never bothered to try to sting him for her maintenance. Perhaps he will feel differently when at long last he gets something published and she claims her fifty per cent.

Meanwhile he takes her across to English's fish restaurant where over a grilled sole and a decent glass of wine Mags relaxes and begins to wax nostalgic, and it slowly becomes apparent that for old times' sake she would not be averse to spending the afternoon in bed with him, if only to keep her out of the pubs and give her something to do until it is time for her 'tech'.

It will be tricky if she wants to come back to his place and Maureen is around. He asks her where she is staying. Not the Grand or the Metropole, he shouldn't think. Royal Albion? Bedford?

'What – on the Equity minimum? You must be joking. No, I'm quite near the Bedford, though. Private hotel called Chilton Court. They give us a special rate.'

The hairs on Duffy's neck bristle. Chilton Court. So called because Chilton was Maureen's mum's name and it is Maureen's maiden name.

Well, it's high time a bit of luck came Duffy's way.

16

Chilton Court has a policy of not handing out front-door keys to its guests, if it can be helped, particularly to theatricals. Theatricals, having during the course of their week in Brighton perhaps had occasion to change their sleeping arrangements to something more accommodating, had the charitable habit of passing on their keys, if they had any, to lesser mortals such as assistant stage managers more unfortunate than themselves, who may until then have been sleeping on someone's floor.

Upon arriving at Chilton Court, therefore, Mags has to ring the doorbell. Duffy is embarrassed and surprised when it is answered by a woman he recognises as Maureen's friend Mrs Cooney.

She is as confused and surprised as he is, for all that she doesn't really know Duffy except through Maureen. The fact that it is only mid-afternoon and broad daylight rather than post-theatre black night is counted by Duffy as a point in his favour. Mumbling something about an old friend from Blackpool and just dropping in for a cup of tea, he follows Mags up the stairs. She is totally unfazed: must have stayed at Chilton Court before.

Duffy feels Mrs Cooney's eyes following them as they ascend to the second floor. He would not put it past her to listen outside Mags's bedroom door. It will get back to

Maureen without doubt – what should he say? Perhaps something approximating the truth. Met ex-wife Mags – she had better remain an ex-wife – outside the Theatre Royal and went back with her to sort out some business about outstanding alimony. Too boring to talk about, if Maureen doesn't mind.

Mags's smallish room, overlooking the back terraces, is furnished from the same 1910 Army & Navy Stores catalogue as Maureen's place in Sheridan Square. The brass bedstead is a single one, but wide enough to serve its purpose.

The tryst is not a brilliant success. Duffy is preoccupied, agitated even, not so much by the unscheduled appearance of Mrs Cooney – he can deal with that when the time comes – as by what to him is the primary purpose of his visit, and the means of bringing it to fruition.

The only way of entering Chilton Court, short of breaking in with a jemmy, is by admission courtesy of Mrs Cooney, so he might just as well get on with it. From the entrance hall he has glimpsed a flight of wooden steps descending to the basement area and, presumably, the cellars. Does Mrs Cooney lurk down there? There is only one way to find out. If she pops out from some pantry or whatever, he will just have to play it by ear.

Such are the thoughts coursing through Duffy's head as he laboriously goes through the motions of making love to his estranged wife. He feels obliged to apologise for being out of practice, which for her part she clearly isn't. Mags feels obliged to tell him that he mustn't put himself down, he can't expect to be as energetic as he was. 'Oh, so I'm a *was* now?' asks Duffy with comic ruefulness. She says 'Oh, do leave off!' and gives him a playful shove.

But never mind all that. This thing has to be done step by step, and step one is to contrive to be left behind in the house when Mags has to go off for her tech rehearsal. He does this by simulating a violent attack of stomach cramps.

Mags, anxious to be away, asks uneasily: 'Are you going to be all right, Chris?'

'I'll be all right when I've spent half an hour on the loo. Go on, Mags – I'll let myself out.'

'Are you sure?'

'I'm sure.' Just bugger off, woman.

'Thanks again for lunch. Are you coming to the show tomorrow?'

'We'll have to see – I don't know what I've got on.'

'Tuesday, then. Or the Wednesday matinee. You can't be tied up all week?'

'I couldn't say for certain, Mags. It's a difficult time – the Brighton Festival.'

'Why, you're not in it, are you?' asks Mags with, to Duffy's mind, offensive incredulity.

'I do have a role,' boasts Duffy. 'You won't find me in the brochure' – this in case she flicks through the brochure out of boredom while awaiting her entrance in the tech – 'but I'm so to speak First Reserve. If someone lets them down, I go in to bat. As I had to do yesterday, interviewing Moss Cody.'

'Who?'

'No, I'd never heard of him either,' says Duffy, gratified. 'But that's the kind of thing I'm doing this week.
It pays the rent.'

'And you won't have one night free to come and see
your doting wife in the best part she's had in years?'
persists Mags.

Duffy is getting irritated. 'Even if I'm not actively
doing anything myself, I have to go and drink in the
Festival. Mix with other writers.'

'Bollocks,' retorts Mags uncouthly.

He is slowly remembering what the problem always
was between them. She never understood writers, as
she always claimed he never understood actors. Didn't
understand the writer's need to spend the evening with
like spirits, the writer's need to be by himself and think,
the writer's need to shag other women, the writer's need
to get pissed. Didn't understand that if writers don't
write, it's because someone else is stopping them.

He had to be away from her then, and he has to be
away from her now. Besides, he has things to do.

Happily, this time round she seems more or less to
understand, although not of course about the things he
has to do.

'If you'll excuse me, Mags, I have to get across to your
bog. Like now.'

'I'll leave the Yale lock off the latch. Do try to come
in, Chris. If not, I suppose I'll see you in another twenty
or thirty years, or however long it's been. It was nice
running into you, darling.'

'You too. Take care.'

He gives her three minutes to get off the premises

and along the promenade and then leaps out of bed and begins to dress. What will he say to Mrs Cooney if she's seen Mags leave and comes up to investigate why Duffy hasn't? Recycle the stomach-cramps story. Mags swallowed it so stick to it.

What if he encounters Mrs Cooney down in the basement? He's come down looking for her, hasn't he? Why? To say goodbye. Why should he want to say goodbye, when he barely knows the woman? All right, to leave a message for Mags. What message? To say he's just remembered, he can't come and see the play tomorrow night, having looked in his diary. Why didn't he write the message down and leave it in her room? Couldn't find a pencil.

By the time he is out on the landing, Duffy has a story for every contingency. He makes his way down the stairs, on tiptoe. Tiptoeing only makes them creak, as they would do. No sign of life. He reaches the basement kitchen. It is empty. He is in luck. With even more luck Mrs Cooney could have gone to the pub or out for a walk on the front.

Across the kitchen is the door to the basement area with the huge key to its mortise lock handily in place. So far, so smooth. Duffy unlocks the door. Opposite it, across the paved area, is the door to the cellars under the street. No key there, but it is unlocked, as he has guessed or anyway hoped it would be. There aren't many Regency properties with the cellar locks still functioning.

Duffy swings open the heavy door and finds a functional-looking light switch. If there's going to be any trouble, here's where it will start. What is he doing in Mrs Cooney's cellar? Looking for her. In the cellar? Come off it! All right, he was looking for her in the kitchen when he thought he heard a cat miaowing in the cellar. Black-and-white kitten. Just now scampered off, poor little thing, could have been in there for days. That should do it. It will have to.

The cellars, two of them, are crammed with the usual detritus to be found in cellars – old lampshades, piles of magazines tied up with string, a broken clothes-horse, a broken ironing board, a broken cocktail trolley, a wind-up gramophone, a vacuum cleaner, no doubt broken like everything else in this bazaar of broken toys. The adjoining cellar, approached through a whitewashed brickwork arch and well under the Brunswick Crescent pavement, is comparatively empty apart from one or two junk-stuffed tea chests and, under the white glare of a naked light-bulb, a handsome leather trunk against the wall. It reminds Duffy so strongly of the trunk in Mister Hamilton's *Rope* as filmed by Mister Hitchcock that he experiences a shudder.

He approaches the trunk and with some hesitation, as if expecting it to contain a body, throws back the creaking lid. A man's pinstriped suit, neatly folded on its wooden hanger. Some shirts in a paper laundry bag, its lettering faded – 'Same-day Par Excellence Service.' Three pairs of shoes. Books. He picks one up. *Fanny by Gaslight*, by Michael Sadleir – undedicated, but no need to ask whose copy it was. A three-quarters-full, or one-quarter-empty, bottle of Scotch. And, beneath a dusty Good Companion portable typewriter and a jumble of blank typing paper, a thick manuscript in fading purple typewriting. Surprisingly, it is unprotected save by a stout but rotting rubber band cutting into its edges, and which when he tries to ease it to stop further tearing of the pages, disintegrates at once.

There is no title page, just the title itself at the top of the first sheet: *Palace Pier*. His heart jumps as he reads the opening sentences:

There are those women who lack morals as bald men lack hair. They are not in themselves immoral, they are not even amoral, any more than one would call a cat amoral. They are simply deficient in moral values, as other women, through none of their own doing, may be lacking in vitamins . . .

A vibration from the pavement above tells Duffy that someone is mounting the front steps and entering the house. Is the cellar light visible from the street? Possibly, or possibly not. At any rate he quickly flicks it off and, hugging the manuscript to his chest, closes the cellar door and is about to cross into the kitchen when he notices, for the first time, a flight of steep steps at the end of the little yard, leading up to the street. He is at them more nimbly than his imaginary black-and-white kitten.

Duffy has been too quick for his own good. As he bounds up the steps to the street he becomes aware that Mrs Cooney, key poised in her gloved hand, is peering down at him from the doorstep.

Has she seen that he has just come out of the cellar? Assume not. He could just as well be coming up from the kitchen.

'Funny way of leaving the house, Mr Duffy. Most of my guests prefer to use the front door.'

'Yes, I was looking for you in the kitchen, Mrs Cooney,' says Duffy glibly. Perhaps too glibly.

Mrs Cooney says tartly: 'There are no cobwebs in my kitchen, Mr Duffy.'

Bugger. 'No,' amends Duffy, brushing the fragment of spider's-web from his sleeve. 'I just put my head round the cellar door to see if you were in there. It was nothing I just wanted to say I was on my way.'

'And you found what you were looking for?'

'Looking for?' echoes Duffy foolishly. Her eyes are fixed on the manuscript clutched to his chest. 'Oh, this? It's a play script that Mags Dodd's asked me to look at. She wants an opinion.'

'Play script,' says Mrs Cooney. 'It doesn't look like a play script to me.'

Duffy is becoming annoyed. What the hell does she know about play scripts? He supposes she means that with its purple type and yellowing paper it looks too old. Wildly, he says: 'It's a revival.'

Mrs Cooney does not purse her lips, but gives the impression of inwardly doing so. 'You realise, Mr Duffy,' she says, 'that I shall have to report this to Maureen?'

Report it? What's she talking about, report it to Maureen? Duffy notices that the man next door has just come home and, under the pretext of searching for his keys, is listening to his neighbour's conversation from his doorstep.

'What's it got to do with Maureen?' he asks.

'That trunk happens to be her property.'

Very probably. But not Mister Patrick Hamilton's belongings. 'She might own the trunk,' he says boldly. 'But not its contents.'

'I wouldn't know about that, Mr Duffy.'

Duffy, suddenly enraged by the inquisitive neighbour, decides to embarrass him as much as he is embarrassed himself. He calls over: 'Excuse me, sir, are you a solicitor by any chance?'

'A solicitor?' The man is startled at being addressed directly. 'No, nothing of that kind.'

'Ah. I thought you might give us an opinion on whether goods left in a house remain the property of their owner or if not reclaimed become the property of the householder.'

'I'm sure this gentleman has no view on that, since he says he isn't a solicitor,' says Mrs Cooney. The neighbour providently discovers that he has been holding his house keys in his hand all along, and swiftly employs them to let himself in. Duffy has no doubt that he continues to listen from behind his front door. Mrs Cooney continues: 'It's something you'll have to have out with Maureen.'

'It's got nothing to do with Maureen,' reiterates Duffy stubbornly.

'Everything that goes on in this house has to do with Maureen,' says Mrs Cooney. 'It should do, seeing as she owns the place.'

Duffy is very surprised. 'I thought you owned it now, Mrs Cooney?'

'Not me, I wish I did, I'm only Maureen's house-keeper. Maureen's a very wealthy woman, that may be something else you don't know,' she adds significantly, as she finally lets herself into Chilton Court.

What is he supposed to make of that? It is probably meant as a threat. Maureen, if he pursues the plan of action he is already outlining in his mind, could in turn perhaps pursue him through the courts.

It will need thinking out. Failing a good lawyer, what Duffy needs is a large drink.

17

But which pub? Mrs Cooney will already be on the blower to Maureen, 'reporting', as she puts it, that he has made away with the manuscript of *Palace Pier*. Maureen will know that he has more sense than to take it home to Sheridan Square. She will guess that his instinct will hone him in on a quiet pub where he can settle down for a good read and a large vodka with a beer chaser.

A veteran of Brighton's pubs, Maureen is familiar with all the ones he uses, except for the Jackdaw, which she refuses to set foot in ever since hearing that it is now used by the garrulous Olive. But Duffy can't go in there either, not when he is carrying the manuscript which Olive is bound to recognise. Not that it's any of her business but it is bound to set her going.

The Pineapple? No way. Swan with Two Necks? Crown and Two Chairmen? Doctor Brighton's? Pavilion Arms? Too risky.

Then he has a brainwave. The Whip Tavern in Trafalgar Street, where Maureen used to work and where he first met her going back years now, is no longer used by Maureen or so she has told him, she having had an altercation with one of her successors. He heads for the Whip Tavern.

It is a fair distance from Chilton Court and it gives

him time to think. The sun is going down and a gust of wind is getting up, blowing across Brunswick Lawns and round the marooned West Pier to the grey sea, which is now going into one of its sullen moods. Duffy cuts through from the seafront into Western Road, heading for Trafalgar Street up Queen's Road past the Clock Tower.

It's another step-by-step exercise. Step one: Ram it home to Maureen, if necessary by putting the fear of God in her, that the manuscript is not her property. No – as you were. Establish first of all that it positively isn't her property, that she couldn't have written it as she outlandishly claims, that it wasn't given to her in lieu of a week's rent, that she has no call upon it. That shouldn't be difficult, not too difficult anyway. Fear of God then becomes step two.

Step three: Explain the difficulties if she insists on clinging on to the manuscript. What difficulties? He'll just have to make some, won't he? Duffy can wing that sort of thing. Step four: Explain his brilliant proposal. Which is? It's coming, it's coming. Duffy is not a creative writer for nothing.

He reaches Trafalgar Street and the Whip Tavern, another of those little pocket-handkerchief pubs so small that if you sneezed you could send the entire clientele home with head colds. That's if there was any clientele: the place is empty except for a scruffy-looking type, mature Sussex University student by the look of him, reading a paperback at a burnished copper table – what must be one of the last such pub tables left in Brighton – over a pint of what is presumably real ale.

There is only one other table in the bar – directly opposite, under the fisherman's-cottage-effect bow window, although Duffy doubts that any fisherman has ever set foot in the place. He sets the manuscript down to establish his claim to the table, then picks it up again and puts it back under his arm. No way is he going to let *Palace Pier* out of his sight. He goes to the bar and orders a pint of somebody or other's Directors' Best Bitter – considering how much he drinks, Duffy is remarkably unselective about what he does drink – and a double, no, make that a treble, vodka, lot of ice, no tonic. The barman, who like the only other customer looks like Sussex University material, gives him an eyebrow-shooting glance but does not otherwise express an opinion.

He conveys the brimming glasses carefully to his copper table, takes a sip of his beer and a deeper swig of his vodka, straightens up the by now folded bundle of typescript, and begins to read:

There are those women who lack morals as bald men lack hair. They are not in themselves immoral, they are not even amoral, any more than one would call a cat amoral . . .

He reads on, beginning already to feel like Lord Carnavon at the mouth of Tutankhamun's tomb:

. . . Such a one was Dorothy Ruth Ferris, the only daughter of a pharmacist and his wife, living, appropriately enough as it was to turn out, in the shadow of Lewes Prison. While at the small private school to which her parents could just afford to send her, Ruth (as she wished to be known,

contemptuously consigning the Dorothy – her mother's maiden name – to the ash heap of history) began, for no discernible reason whether psychological, pathological or traumatic, and after two blemishless terms during which the only black mark against her was a charge of shoving at netball, to get into the habit of helping herself to small sums of money or other items she came across while compulsively rifling the pockets of garments hanging in the cloakroom.

For these sneak-thief activities, her parents having refused point-blank to listen to what Ruth's headmistress Felt It Her Duty to tell them, Ruth was ultimately expelled. Thus, at the earliest age, she was set upon what was still known, in some quarters and at that time, as the Road to Ruin . . .

Another gulp of vodka, another glug of beer, and Duffy goes on reading, although he doesn't have to. All Mister Hamilton's trademark characteristics are there already. The discursive, third-person-once-removed, sociological-type opening. The leisurely beginning to the narrative. The overuse of what, as Duffy remembers Mister Priestley complaining of in his introduction to one of Mister Hamilton's novels, Komic Kapitals. Even – so far a private theory of Duffy's, this, which he could drum up into a bit of a thesis given any encouragement – that in his later work it is possible to spot how Mister Hamilton had begun to write in 1,000-word spurts, after which the urge to get down the pub took over from the creative impulse. And—

'Excuse me, are you by any chance an author?'

He looks up to find the only other occupant of the

bar, the mature student character, looming over him, clutching a pint glass.

It is a question Duffy has not been asked in years, not in fact since he left Blackpool, where anyone seen with a pen in his top pocket may be taken for a writer.

Despite the interruption, he is flattered. 'Why do you ask?' he hedges politely – coyly, as a cynical observer might put it.

'Only you look like one, that's all.'

The interloper continues to loiter, evidently expecting a more substantial reply to his enquiry. Duffy says: 'Since you do ask, I do happen to be a writer, yes.' He just manages to stop short of adding: 'For my sins.'

'What do you write, then?'

Christ, how long ago is it since he was last asked this unanswerable, imbecile question? And what did he used to reply?

'Anything that comes into my head.'

'So do you just walk about, like, till you've thought up something to write about, then you write it all down?'

Duffy demotes the man from mature student to comprehensive-school caretaker. 'Something like that, yes.'

The man nods sagely and returns, thank God, to the bar. Relieved, Duffy picks up his manuscript again.

... Ruth's drift into prostitution, at the comparatively mature age of seventeen, was, like many such journeys, a deceptively smooth expedition ...

'And is that a book that you've written?'

Oh, God, the bugger is back. He's only been up to the bar for a refill.

'Yes. A novel,' says Duffy curtly.

Please, please, please, don't let him ask: 'And is it going to be published?' Or: 'How do you set about writing a novel, I wouldn't know where to begin?' Or: 'How long did it take you to write it?' Or: 'Do you do it in longhand first and then type it up?' Or: 'Do they ask you to write it or do you just send it in and hope for the best?'

None of these. Even worse: 'What's it about?'

At least he has a reply to that poser. He remembers it from his Blackpool days. 'If I could tell you that in a few words, I wouldn't have bothered writing the book.'

To Duffy's horror his interrogator now takes the adjoining stool at the burnished copper table. 'You don't mind if I join you, do you?'

What can he say? 'Yes, I do, actually. Intensely'? He has not got the nerve. He shrugs, buries his face in *Palace Pier* with an expression of deep concentration, and hopes the intruder will take the hint.

The intruder doesn't. 'Do you mind if I ask you a question?'

Duffy sighs with elaborate rudeness. 'Go on.'

'You're sure you don't mind?'

'No, I don't mind.' Duffy looks significantly at his watch.

'Why do you type out your books in purple?'

So it is that, mumbling something about having to get to the local BBC studio for an interview with the *South Coast Show* ('You do a lot of interviews, do you? Do you always know what to say?'), he is driven out of the pub.

Thus he makes for an obscure-looking pub in a side-street near the Theatre Royal, not realising until he is halfway through a much-needed large vodka that he has stumbled inside the little-used back entrance of the Pavilion Arms.

And thus it is, absorbed in the manuscript of *Palace Pier*, that he falls into the clutches of Maureen.

18

The story, like much of Mister Hamilton's work, seems deceptively straightforward. Her father by this time dead, Ruth moves with her mother to Brighton. The widow now having her own preoccupations, Ruth is allowed a long rein.

One summer evening she is playing the slot machines on the Palace Pier when she is accosted by a businessman, a traveller in seaside novelties, who takes her across to one of the hotels for a cocktail. Ruth quickly becomes squiffy.

Unnoticed by her, it turns out that her mother is in the cocktail bar, being entertained by a gentleman friend (Ruth's mother has a frisky side which is developing in widowhood). While Ruth absents herself in the Ladies', her mother comes across and introduces herself. Does the businessman realise, she asks boldly, that her daughter is under-age? (She isn't, but from her youthful appearance she might well be.) The businessman protests the innocence of his intentions. But it is not long, such is his lust, before money changes hands.

Thus is established a mother-and-daughter double act. Ruth picks up men on the Palace Pier and takes them across to the cocktail bar and subsequently to the victim's hotel room or back to her home. Her mother intervenes. They split the proceeds.

This goes on until Ruth meets a married wholesaler of rock and confectionery on Palace Pier, with whom she happens to fall hopelessly in love. The bulk of the story is then concerned with her attempts to get her weak-minded lover out of the clutches of her mother . . .

Duffy is so gripped by the narrative that it is not for some minutes that he becomes aware of the altercation in the other bar – the other bar being the larger front bar of the Pavilion Arms which is the one he customarily uses. Duffy has found himself in the small back bar, what in the old days would have been called the Snug, which is connected to the main bar by a small serving hatch.

It is through this serving hatch that he has in the back of his mind been hearing raised voices. 'Smarrer wi' yew, ven, nosy old cah? Want some, do we, ma? Cause if yer do, yer stewpid cah . . .'

'Leave it, mate. She don't want none, do ya, ma? Cause she knows what she'll get if she starts, know worramin . . . ?'

Then the aggrieved woman's voice: 'Don't you talk to me like that, or.' Followed by: 'And don't think I don't know your names, so.'

Shit. Gallantry has never been Duffy's strong suit, but he can hardly leave Maureen to whatever her fate might be. Especially since the barman is now saying: 'All right, lads, leave it out,' and the first of the aggressors, the more drunken of the two, is slurring: 'Lea it aht? Lea it aht? Lea yew aht, cant!'

With an inward sigh Duffy, the script of *Palace Pier* still under his arm, pushes through the pass door into the main bar. Maureen is looking defiant but frightened.

Two old gaffers, nursing half-pints across the room, are studiously pretending to have heard nothing, seen nothing. They are the only occupants besides Maureen and the two yobs, one of whom is insolently sprawled across a banquette with his feet up, the other in the tripping position for anyone who happens to walk by.

At a glance, Duffy can see that nothing on the lines of 'Excuse me, would you two mind moderating your language?' is going to work. He says what the barman should have said minutes ago: 'You. Out.'

'Woss say?' enquires one yob of the other, over-gormlessly.

'You're annoying this lady with your language,' says Duffy. 'So piss off, why don't you?'

'Else what?' scoffs the more sober of the two. The more drunken one, to Duffy's relief, already looks prepared to call it a day.

As his contribution to the spat, the barman comes round and holds open the street door. 'Now then, lads, I'm not serving you any more, so you might as well go.' Mouthing obscenities and jabbing 'Up you' gestures in the barman's face, the drunks stagger out to make a nuisance of themselves elsewhere.

One of the old gaffers shakes his head in a what's-the-world-coming-to manner. The other says, to the room at large: 'I don't know. I don't. I do not.' What promises to be an inquest into the altercation is cut short by Maureen, who pragmatically says to Duffy: 'Well, after all that, I expect you could do with a.'

Meanwhile Duffy has now realised, in retrospect, what has been happening to his copy of *Palace Pier* in all the confusion. He has put the manuscript down upon Maureen's table in anticipation of any fisticuffs that might occur. Maureen has picked it up, identified it, and now clutches it proprietorially to her bosom. She continues to clutch it as she shuffles the couple of steps to the bar to order Duffy's drink, and she does not relinquish it as she resumes her seat.

Rather than allow Maureen to make the running, Duffy decides to go on the offensive himself, and at once.

'Now, Maureen, you're not going to be silly, are you?'

'Silly, I don't know what you.'

'That manuscript isn't your property and you know it.'

'It certainly isn't yours, Chris!' retorts Maureen, permitting herself a fully-rounded sentence in her indignation.

'To begin with, you didn't write it.'

'Oh, but I did.'

'Oh, but you didn't.'

The two old gaffers brooding over their half-pints pretend not to be listening, but their eyes swivel this way and that, as at a tennis tournament. If the row heats up, reflects Duffy, perhaps they may be needed as witnesses.

These did-didn't exchanges go on at length until the argument is moved on a notch by Maureen saying: 'All right, you prove I didn't. If.'

But Duffy has already worked on this one on the walk from Chilton Court: 'Maureen. Don't take my word for it – there are people who know about these things. Experts. Critics. Literary analysts.' What is a literary analyst? Luckily, Maureen doesn't ask.

Duffy taps the manuscript which by now is back on neutral ground on Maureen's table. 'These days they can feed this stuff into a computer, Maureen, compare it with other samples of Mister Hamilton's work, and prove beyond any shadow of doubt who the true author really is.'

This sounds convincing enough. At any rate it seems to convince Maureen, who falls silent. Duffy presses home his advantage:

'And even if you did get away with it, Maureen, think about when it's published, under your name. The interviews. The publicity. The questions. Why did you hang back all these years before publishing?'

'I've told you, because there were living people involved. So. I didn't like to.'

'Don't tell me what you liked or didn't like, Maureen. It's what you've got to tell a packed audience at next year's Brighton Festival. Local audience? They'll be down from the *Guardian*, the *Indie*, *The Times*, *Sunday Times* – they'll crucify you. Make mincemeat of you. Believe you me, you won't get out of that Corn Exchange alive.'

Duffy is ready to go on in this threatening vein for some minutes but Maureen has already put up the white flag. But for an armistice, not an unconditional surrender.

'If you say so, Chris, but it's still my.'

'Still your book? How can you make that out?' Is

Maureen stupid, or what? Well, since Duffy asks this of himself, yes, she is.

'Because I told it to him, didn't I? All he did was to write it down. So.'

What emerges, from Maureen's disjointed sentences, is that while staying with Maureen and her mother so long ago at Chilton Court, Mister Hamilton asked with mild curiosity about some of the contents of the wardrobe in his room, casually discovered. Certain garments. Maureen doesn't specify, but at a guess they would be rubber, leather, fishnet, fur-lined handcuffs – quite advanced for those days. But her answers to Mister Hamilton's questions led her – the story doubtless being dragged out of her like a Caesarean delivery – to tell him something about her young life. It's as Duffy thought. *Palace Pier* is about, or at the very least inspired by, Maureen's early life.

'So,' reiterates Maureen in triumph.

Duffy delivers a short lecture on the laws of copyright, insofar as he knows anything about them, and then proceeds to what he hopes will be more fertile ground.

'But the question is, Maureen, where do we go from here?'

'We?' asks Maureen sharply.

'Cards-on-table time, Maureen,' says Duffy briskly, having got in another round. 'There are three things you can do with this novel. You can hand it over to the Hamilton Estate, whoever they may be. Whatever they do with it, there's no reason for them to give you sod-all – it's their property. Two, you can publish it as your own work, with all the risks I've explained. Or.'

Conscious that he is replicating Maureen's own speech pattern, Duffy pauses for dramatic effect.

'Or what?'

'Or you could publish it under someone else's name.'

'Whose?'

Deep-breath time. 'Mine.'

Duffy has thought all this out too, even when the real authorship of *Palace Pier* was but a glimmer of a suspicion, when he was still ransacking Maureen's flat in search of the manuscript. This evening, between Chilton Court, the Whip Tavern and the Pavilion Arms, he has his master plan polished to perfection.

He will get the manuscript retyped overnight. Not in purple. First thing tomorrow morning he will get round to the Pier Lodge Hotel and place it in the hands of that literary agent Gregory Coates, who has shown such an interest in his work and whose business card is in his top pocket.

Pier Lodge. Hm. By now Duffy has set eyes on the place. Bit of a dump, as Gregory freely admitted. But if he was having to pay his own way he couldn't be expected to stump up Metropole or Grand Hotel prices. And *Palace Pier* would be a bit of a coup for him.

So why is it a period piece? Because of changing mores, changing morals. Yes, but 1962? He has been suffering from writer's block. With a client-list like his, Gregory must know the feeling.

And when the book comes out? Chris Duffy's long-awaited second novel, transferring his beat from Blackpool to Brighton? What will they make of the undoubted influence? There are clear indications that Mister Duffy has been rereading his Patrick Hamilton, but none the worse for that. Yes, he should be able to get away with that.

But Maureen is ahead of him. 'You're saying they'd make mincemeat of me if I tried to pass it off as my. What about you trying to pass it off as your?'

And he's even further ahead of her. He's practised this speech, on the walk over from Chilton Court. Got it word-perfect. 'Maureen. I'm an established, published writer. Compared with Mister Jack Trevor Story in one review. Plus, I've got another novel of my own in my drawer back at the flat, just crying out to be published. You can read it if you like.'

'So why should you want to?'

'Because I need a credit, Maureen. A kick-start. Through no fault of my own I haven't published anything for a while. This would give me the impetus I need. Re-establish my credentials.'

'And you reckon you could?'

'Get away with it? Of course I could get away with it. Do it in my sleep. Wing it. You know me, Maureen.'

She does, too. Maureen's not as dim as Duffy seems to think. She can see the whole picture. *Palace Pier*, by Chris Duffy. From the author of *Razzle-Dazzle*.

'So what's in it for?' asks Maureen shrewdly.

'I don't know, Maureen. What would you want?

'Half the doings,' says Maureen firmly. 'What are they called? Royalties. Or.'

Jesus. 'There's a lot of editing to do,' protests Duffy, weakly.

'They have their own editors to do that, these

publishers do. So,' says Maureen. She has been reading too many writing-school brochures.

So, then. Fifty per cent of the takings to Maureen. Plus the other fifty per cent he's already promised to Mags. Or rather, she's promised it to herself.

Easy come. Duffy doesn't give a toss. He gets a hundred per cent of the credit. That's what matters.

19

Not one to let the grass grow, at least not on this particular plot, Duffy gives Maureen a couple of minutes to take herself off, undoubtedly to Chilton Court, there to compare notes with Mrs Cooney on whatever else he might have got away with out of Mister Hamilton's old trunk. That *Fanny by Gaslight*, for instance. Michael Sadleir, big pal of Hamilton's. It had to be a first edition. He wishes he'd taken it now. Got to be worth something.

He zips the manuscript of *Palace Pier* inside his bomber jacket before setting off for Pier Lodge. He has decided against getting the script retyped: it would take three girls hammering away all night to get the job done, and it would cost a bomb, even if that secretarial bureau over the tattoo and piercing centre in West Street were open on a Sunday evening, which it won't be. He is certainly too pissed to type out the thing himself, and proposes to get even more pissed as the evening wears on.

What he will do, he will get it photocopied first thing in the morning. With the tell-tale purple replaced by black, and the yellowing quarto typing paper translated into white and shining A4, it will look as if it could have been completed this weekend. New title page: PALACE

PIER a novel by CHRIS DUFFY. The right of Christopher Duffy to be identified as the author of this work has been asserted by him in accordance with the Copyright, Designs and Patents Act 1988.

Pier Lodge looks even grottier by twilight than when he walked past to give it the once-over during daylight hours. Basically, like several similar establishments in the shabby side-street – Ferndale, the Royale, Bide-a-While – it consists of two pebbledash late Edwardian villas bashed into one, doubtless with room dividers made of fibreboard. The lingering smell of some unidentifiable soup or stew with ozone undertones reminds him of Blackpool.

And Gregory Coates isn't in. He had an early supper, the first sitting, and went out for the evening. Took a key with him, so most likely gone off to one of them Brighton Festival events and won't be back till late.

Jesus Christ, is the poor bastard on full board in this dump? Not for the first time, Duffy has misgivings about his choice of literary agent. Not that he did choose this Gregory Coates – Gregory Coates chose him. He has in fact been humiliatingly turned down by half a dozen agents over the years:

'Sorry, old man, we just can't take on anyone else at this moment in time.'

'Sorry, old chap, in the present climate we've got to be so choosy about what new fiction we take on board, you know how it is.'

'Sorry, old friend, you're at the wrong end of the time-scale for the kind of market we're targeting.'

'Dear Mr Duffle, I have been asked to acknowledge your letter but with regret . . .'

Sorry, chum.

Duffy leaves a message for Gregory Coates that he will be back at breakfast-time, this on the assumption that Coates will be returning to London first thing. He does give the impression of having a day job of some kind. The slattern who has answered the door does not convince Duffy that the message will ever be delivered. He will just have to be on the doorstep at the crack of half past nine or thereabouts, *Palace Pier* under one arm and *The Golden Mile*, that's if he can find it after all this time, under the other. Probably it has made its way into one of Olive's carrier bags by now. If not, he will go for a two-book deal.

Duffy hurries down the scruffy little street to the front, where he is met by an icy gust of wind coming in from the west and blowing out to sea. It is getting chilly now. He heads for the warming yellow lights of the Hotel Metropole. A tincture in the glassed-in seafront bar would be just the thing, preferably with Dizzy Lizzie, if she's around.

But she isn't. Nobody is, of any consequence. Where is this Festival that's supposed to be going on? Where is the action? He wanders aimlessly about the hotel's near-deserted lobby, and then departs in favour of the Grand next door.

But as he's leaving, he spots a young couple coming away from the bar area and heading for the lifts, hand in hand. He goes twice around the revolving doors to establish their identity. Dizzy Lizzie and Moss Cody, and not only hand in hand but entangled like octopuses.

Duffy feels unaccountably depressed. Unaccountably, because what the fuck has it got to do with him? Moss Cody, successful writer, is well within her best-screw-by-age range, which Duffy is way beyond, and the fact that she gave him one-night-stand rights on a bored evening when there was nothing better on offer does not convey a long-term or even short-term involvement in her own affairs.

Did she see him? It's possible, although she does not acknowledge the fact, and specifically, does not cease entwining her ankles around Cody's. Moss Cody almost certainly didn't. He is not the kind of personality who goes around noticing people. How in God's name did he get to call himself a writer?

Duffy turns sharp left to make the few yards to the Grand Hotel, where he intends to invest fourteen pounds on the biggest, stiffest vodka martini he has ever seen in his life. Or anyway, a fourteen-pound martini. After that he proposes to get rat-arsed.

He has reached the entrance to the Grand when he hears the clack-clack of hurrying high-heel sandals and a cry of: 'Duffy! Duffy!'

Nobody calls him Duffy except his best friends, and he doesn't have any best friends. Worst enemies, perhaps. But she certainly doesn't come under that heading, not that he's aware of.

'Duffy, have you a minute? I want to say sorry.'

For what? For being spotted?

He shrugs his lips. Magnanimously, he hopes. 'A

minute earlier, a minute later, and I wouldn't have seen you.'

'I know, but it's not my bad timing I'm apologising for.'

'Why should you? As you say yourself, it's what you do.'

'You don't understand. He's one of our authors.'

'Oh, I *see*!' He lays on the irony with a trowel.

'No, you don't see, Duffy. It's my job to amuse them. I've been so busy looking after Anna May Beeston that I've been completely neglecting him. Very least I can do.'

And what, Duffy idly wonders, is this very least she can do? Blow-job? He doesn't ask.

'So what is it you're sorry about?'

'Oh – that you're not one of our authors,' says Dizzy Lizzie lightly, but with meaning.

Duffy, trying but failing to give the same soufflé-like touch to his response, says: 'You never know. Since you ask, I'm delivering a novel to my agent tomorrow morning.'

'What's it called? Are you pleased with it?'

'It's called *Palace Pier* and yes I am. It should make me a *with* again.'

'A what?'

'A *with*. It's a joke I have with my ex.' He thinks that Mags had better remain his ex-wife even though it now appears that she isn't. Laboriously, he explains the *with-and-but* joke. 'So in theatrical billing terms, I may never have my name in lights but I do aspire to be a *with*.'

Quick on the uptake, Lizzie understands first time round. 'Better than being an *of*, anyway.'

'Of? Of what?'

'*Of* whoever I happen to be working for. All my life I've been an *of*. Lizzie of Blah Blah Productions. Lizzie of Blah Blah Presentations. Lizzie of Blah Blah Publications. Always the bridesmaid, never the bride.'

Her mini-diatribe does make the case for hopping into bed with clients, which would seem to be her hobby. If you're nobody, reasons Duffy, it must help to be somebody for an hour or two.

'Will you read my book, if and when it sees the light?' he asks.

'Of course I will. Who do you say your agent is again?'

'I didn't, but it's Gregory Coates.'

He speaks with diffidence, knowing instinctively that she will not approve.

'Gregory Coates is a prat. Can't you do better than that?'

'I don't know, I haven't tried.'

'Do you ever come up to London?'

'Yes – tomorrow,' says Duffy, a touch too eagerly.

'Come and have a drink at the Grouch. Call me.'

He doesn't dare ask where the Groucho Club is, never having crossed its threshold. It'll be in the book. ('Who's the oldish guy with Lizzie? Guy pouring the champagne?' 'I *think* it's her new squeeze. Chris Duffy. *Palace Pier*, this month's dark horse. She brought it in.')

Dizzy Lizzie cuts into his reverie: 'I've got to go back. I told Moss I'd left my mobile down in the bar. If I'm much longer he'll be ringing me up on it.'

On cue, her mobile tinkles. Blowing Duffy a kiss and clattering away on her high heels she answers it: 'Sorree, darling, they couldn't find where they'd put it. In the fridge of all places. I'm on my way up . . .'

Why has Moss bloody Cody got her mobile number and Duffy hasn't, especially considering that she has asked him to call her tomorrow? Call her where? Clearly a proficient liar, she'll be out. 'Lizzie is not at her desk at present, but if you would like to post an email . . .' From being elated he is plunged into gloom again. Can these abrupt mood-swings be accounted for by his drinking? Whether they can or not, he now proposes to have that large one in the Grand Hotel.

The Grand's lobby too is sparsely populated, save a gaggle of young things in evening dress, who look more Young Farmers' Club than Brighton Festival. Where the hell is everybody?

There is a hovering young man in a leather-patched sports jacket who, clutching a half of lager, has the air of a wannabe writer who has been left behind by his friends. Or dumped. Duffy has the option of cutting him dead or taking him up and patronising him. 'Yes, they do say it's tough at the top, but that's easy enough to say when you're up there. It's tough at the bottom, too, and believe me, son, I've been there . . .' Duffy becomes aware that his lips are moving as the young man turns and stares fixedly at a sepia view of Volk's Electric Railway.

Sod him: Duffy has things to do. He's still got a

hundred pages or so of this bloody manuscript to plough through. He can hardly hand over the script of his own novel – to Dizzy Lizzie rather than Gregory Coates, of course – before he has read it himself, now can he?

He gulps down his jumbo-size vodka martini and wanders, or rather staggers, along past the bleak Conference Centre and up to the Festival Club. Surely to Christ there must be somebody here he knows?

Nobody – not even his hurrying, scurrying, brochure-clasping, over-organising friend Pol Crosby, to whom he has been hoping to say: 'Sorry, darling, tomorrow no can do, I'd love to stand in for Master Amis but I've got to get up to London for drinkies with my publisher.'

Not a soul. It is as if the seafront watering holes were a flotilla of landlocked Marie Celestes. Then a glance at the Festival 'What's On' noticeboard tells him all. Some VIP American bugger – the name oozes out of his memory as quickly as it has just oozed into it, but the bugger is on a par with Mister Updike or Mister Gore Vidal – is speaking 'in conversation with', which is to say he doesn't have to do any homework, someone deferentially his British junior, although something of a name in his own right. This is at the Brighton Dome Concert Hall. House full. Charming. No one invited Duffy. He feels as he did when a child, excluded from some mate's birthday party.

Next year, next year . . . All right, perhaps not the Dome Concert Hall, but what's wrong with the Pavilion Theatre? House full, more or less. Moss bloody Cody to do the interview. 'Chris, it's been a long gap between novels.' 'It has been a long gap, Moss, deliberately a very long gap, but without comparing oneself with Mister Salinger . . .' Or perhaps not.

He does not have another zonko, which is what he affably calls his treble vodka martini at this hour, in the hope that they will sound more consumer-friendly to whoever might be serving them. He does not wish to be found slumped over the bar like that character in Mister Hamilton's *Hangover Square*, the one who gassed himself.

One thing: Duffy has nothing to gas himself for. Tomorrow, up at cracko, round the photocopying bureau, cappuccino, croissant and the *Guardian* at the Trois Mages while they're running it off, fast train to Victoria, call Dizzy Lizzie from the station, maybe she can do lunch? No, don't sound too eager, Duffy. Stick to the arrangement as is. Mooch along Charing Cross Road, locate the Groucho, couple of pubs, call her up.

Should he go and live in London? It's to be thought about. He's rather had Brighton, and he doesn't fancy Maureen breathing down his neck when *Palace Pier* comes out, doing a spoiler on his publicity like that prat of a deck-chair attendant up in Blackpool over *Razzle-Dazzle*. Earl's Court he could live in – Hangover Square. Soho. Chelsea. He will have to see.

Where do writers hang out in London? Those clubs he's read about? Certain pubs, certain restaurants, certain cafés? He's never bothered to find out. Well, perhaps 'bothered' is the wrong word – he's never had any wish to find out, until the time was ripe, until London was ready for him. He didn't want to be like that poor geek back in the Grand, sipping his half of lager and looking for someone to talk to him. No, when he arrives in London, it will be in style, an arrival to remember. Turn again, turn again, thrice on the best-seller lists. *The South Bank Show* – is that still on? Profile in the *Guardian* – Chris Duffy talks to Moss Cody. That feature in the *Indie* – 'You Ask the Questions.' *I read, Chris, that you binned your last novel because you thought it wasn't up to scratch. Is that rigorous practice one you'd recommend to aspiring authors . . . ?*

Enough of this day-dreaming. First things first: half a bottle of vodka before the wine shops close. Then what, or rather then where? Still too early for the Festival Club, where in any case after last night's performance he can probably consider himself banned. He doesn't want to go back to the flat in case Maureen has changed her mind and wants the manuscript back. In fact there's a good case to be made for not going back until she's well asleep, and being off the premises in the morning long before she stirs.

Half-bottle in hand, he establishes himself in a shelter on the windy esplanade and drags the manuscript out of his bomber jacket. The blurred purple type is impossible to read, particularly since he's beginning to see double unless he closes one eye.

He could go over to one of the seafront pubs but everyone will be half-cut by now and someone will say: 'What you reading, mate? Is it a book? Why isn't it in proper printing?'

Across from the promenade the thousands of electric light bulbs that outline the gleaming white filigree ironwork of the Palace Pier's arches, turrets, pillars and pavilions wink and twinkle in the breeze. The pier looks cheery and welcoming, and at this late hour it should not be too crowded. Easy to find a cosy, well-lit spot where Duffy can read and glug his vodka in peace. Maybe he can put his hands on a hamburger or something before the pier puts the shutters up. He cannot remember when he last ate. Oh, yes, lunch at English's with Mags. Was that today?

He makes his way over to the pier. There's no admission charge these days and so they've taken away the turnstiles. The consequence is that a tribe of restless urchins, like grounded starlings, are larking about around the entrance to the pier. There has been a drum-beating Festival conga-line sashaying along Marine Parade and in their ragged way they are trying to emulate it. Although they should have been in bed hours ago, Duffy is indulgent, while determining to give them a wide berth.

Led by a boy banging a dustbin lid with a stick, the conga-line weaves off around a ricochet-echoing slot-machine arcade. Accordingly Duffy veers to the opposite side of the pier, the side sheltered from the stiff south-westerly breezes. He treads almost the entire length of the pier, stopping only momentarily for a sip from his flat half-bottle. Towards the pierhead, where anglers foregather when the tide is in, he finds a well-sheltered bench overlooking the sea, and sits down.

Duffy has been doing some desultory thinking. In the course of the long evening he believes he has probably pinpointed where the script of his unpublished novel *The Golden Mile* is, or rather was. When he headed south from Blackpool, light-years ago now, he left behind at his by then widowed mother's the box that was his equivalent of Mister Hamilton's trunk over at Chilton Court. And in it was almost certainly the script of *The Golden Mile* which he'd always meant to send for or go up and retrieve, but he never had. And of course his mother was long dead by this time and the house sold or more likely pulled down, and that script along with his other meagre possessions dispersed into the North Atlantic winds. Good.

This is what he will do now. Starting tomorrow – all right, Tuesday, Wednesday, whenever he's back from London and over the Groucho equivalent of jet lag, he will begin at once on an entirely new novel. The sequel to *Palace Pier*, or rather not so much a sequel as a companion volume – the identical story, but told from the man's point of view. Maybe a third volume, looking at it from the girl's mother's angle. Why not? It's just the kind of thing Mister Hamilton might have done himself, had he ever published *Palace Pier* under his own name – he did have a weakness for trilogies. Why let a good story with good characters go to waste? It will write itself. After that, as a re-established writer, Duffy will just wait for the commissions to roll in. Christmas short story? When do you want it?

He takes a deep gulp of vodka and shuffles the purple-printed pages into a neat stack.

Why is he so reluctant to resume his reading? He will know soon enough. He knows already.

20

Who should be hanging around the far end of the pier but his erstwhile agent, Gregory Coates, quite obviously in the hope of finding female company. Cruising, is the way Duffy would put it. This does not embarrass him so much as the fact that Gregory has yet to realise he is erstwhile.

He has not seen Duffy, who cringes back in the shadow thrown by the bench on which he has established himself. Presently Coates, giving a fair impression of someone wearing a grubby raincoat even though he is not, slinks off down the pier.

Relieved, Duffy smoothes out the manuscript and delves into it approximately at where he left it.

Dorothy Ruth Ferris, by now hopelessly in love, goes up to London to locate her beloved's garden-village home, not with the object of making trouble but with the innocent intention of feasting her eyes masochistically upon his superior well-built semi-detached villa, five mins District Railway, and with any luck catching a glimpse of his equally well-built suburban wife, in the hope of finding her the joyless creature as described by her lover:

Shepherds Pond Drive could well be renamed Philanderers Row. The dozen or so mild-mannered, clerkly-looking householders, most of them moustached and billycocked, and all of them briefcased and brollied, who emerge from its sunburst garden gates each weekday morning and walk briskly, like so many clockwork men, to their Metro-land station, could only be English poisoners, or English adulterers, or both . . .

Then it hits him, the *Click!* inside the head, 'the sound which a noise makes when it abruptly ceases', which occurs in the opening lines of Mister Hamilton's novel *Hangover Square*.

It is the realisation, the confirmation rather, of something he knows very well he has known all along.

It is like finally discovering, proof positive, that a wife is unfaithful even though one has already amassed enough evidence to drag her through the divorce courts.

It is like walking on to a concert-hall platform, sitting at the Bechstein and finding to one's amazement, even while keenly conscious of never having had a piano lesson, that one can only play 'Chopsticks'.

It is like being invited to take the wheel of a girl-friend's Alfa 156 and having to confess at last that one cannot drive.

Duffy cannot write.

Well, dilute that. He can pass muster. But he is in the cuckolded-by-the-milkman, upright cottage piano, Morris Minor league. He is, or was, publishable – just. But he is not, has never been, and if he lives to write a million words never will be, in the class of the man whose stuff he has been reading. He could not go one round with Mister Hamilton.

And this is not even vintage Hamilton. In fact Mister Hamilton's last, as this must be, is Mister Hamilton's worst, if Duffy is any judge.

It figures. Written when – 1961? He was seriously on the sauce by then. The whisky diet. He had, Maureen had told Duffy in confidence, having learned it in equal confidence from her mother, a habit of pouring Scotch into his morning tea and gin into his tooth glass. Some evenings, she'd said, or rather some afternoons, for it got so he rarely made it to the evening, he had to be helped to bed.

All this is fine by Duffy. The roll-call of practised piss-artists in literature was a long one. Mister Fitzgerald, Mister Hemingway, Mister Chandler, Mister Hammett, Mizz Parker. Why, in passing, were they mainly Americans? Prohibition, he supposes. But booze didn't affect their work. Here, in this purple typescript, is evidence that it affected Mister Hamilton.

Duffy, reading on, can by now tell, because he has pulled the same trick himself, how Mister Hamilton would force himself to write a thousand words before rewarding himself with a stiff one. He can tell whether he then went back to work or left it at that for the day, for when he did go back it deteriorated. It deteriorates anyway, as the manuscript wears on. Mister Hamilton has lost it.

But if Mister Hamilton has lost it, then it is plain even from these substandard pages that Duffy has never found it.

Duffy remembers – no, he doesn't remember, he retains, like a fishbone in the throat, a passage from Mister James M. Cain's *The Postman Always Rings Twice* which he chanced to be reading when the postman rang once and the rejected script of *The Golden Mile* came back for the sixth and final time.

He still has that green Penguin edition on his bookshelves. Shelf singular that should be – most of his books have been sold down the years. There's a quote from a review on the back cover that says Mister Cain is better than most of Mister Hemingway. Duffy will drink to that.

And the passage that will remain forever stuck in his gullet is where the broad is explaining to the guy how she came to marry this Greek slob and finish up in a roadside sandwich joint. She won a high-school beauty contest and the prize was a Hollywood screen test. Duffy can still quote it verbatim:

'They talk, now. The pictures, I mean. And when I began to talk, up there on the screen, they knew me for what I was, and so did I. A cheap Des Moines trollop, that had as much chance in pictures as a monkey has . . .'

Why has he remembered that, all these years? Story of his life, that's why. The books he'd been brought up with didn't talk. Mister Priestley, Mister Bennett, Mister Galsworthy, they wrote silent novels – good in their way but he could have gone fifteen rounds with any one of those authors, as writers then were called. But then into Duffy's life came Mister Fitzgerald with, to his mind, fiction's equivalent of *The Jazz Singer*.

Knockout. You hadn't heard nuthin' yet, at least Duffy hadn't, and at heart he knew himself for what he was, a flash-in-the-pan Blackpool scribbler.

He should have stayed with the dodgems on the Golden Mile.

He's beginning to see where he took the wrong turning. He should've become a pulp writer. *Sexton Blake and the Case of the Limping Man.*

This calls for a stiff one. In the plural, because what ensues is going to be important to Duffy, although he doesn't know it yet.

When he comes to look back upon this sequence of events he will see it in slow motion, perhaps not comprehending that it was in slow motion that it actually happened.

A stiff wind is blowing up in gusts from the South Downs along the steep streets leading towards the shore. To free his hands so as to get at his half-bottle of Smirnoff, Duffy lays the manuscript on the bench beside him. He may be fuddled but he is not a fool. The pages need weighting, otherwise they will be ruffled by the breeze and could even blow away. He could sit on them but that would crease them. He settles for pegging them down with his half-bottle of vodka.

Thus in solving one problem he has created another. For how does he open the half-bottle which is now anchoring the pages?

Good question, but he can solve it. He picks up the half-bottle and with his free hand secures the wad of manuscript.

He will open the half-bottle with his teeth. No, he

won't, because in the first place his teeth are not up to it. He does not wish to report to Dizzy Lizzie at the Groucho with a set of stumps where his rotting molars used to be. Secondly, he has remembered that Mister Tennessee Williams died from choking on a pill bottle he was trying to open with his teeth.

He replaces the half-bottle on the pages and looks around him for some alternative heavy object. Through the floorboards of the pier he can see the white spume of the swirling tide. There is a squall building up. You would think there would be a bit of washed-up driftwood, flotsam, jetsam, something of the kind, lying around. Nothing.

The breeze, now angrily changing direction, warns him not to let go of his precious manuscript for a second. Hand firmly pressed down to augment the weight of the vodka flask, he levers off his right shoe with his left foot. Imitation Nike trainers. Are they heavy enough? Should be.

He gropes for the shoe as a gust flutters the pages of *Palace Pier* around its half-bottle paperweight. He shuffles it over the manuscript and retrieves the half-bottle. Well and good. The pages flap and crackle restlessly but the mock-Nike has them secure. It will leave a studded footprint on page one but that can't be helped.

He now has the half-bottle gripped in his trembling hands – they are trembling because it has been a fraught interlude – and is anxious, no, desperate, to get at its contents.

But that's easier said than done. After his last swig of vodka he must have replaced the screw cap carelessly, in his hurry to secure it. Why he should have been in a hurry to replace the cap, rather than the other way round, he cannot explain to himself, but the consequence is that he has somehow fouled the thread of the bottle-neck, leaving him only with the option of biting off the top of the bottle in the manner of – was it Ray Milland in *The Lost Weekend*?

Before Duffy can consider his position further there is a commotion behind him as the urchin conga procession, having circuited the various arcades and pavilions, straggles along in the direction of the pierhead. Their leader, having dropped or tossed into the sea his dustbin-lid makeshift drum, is on the lookout for further distractions. He sees Duffy's scuffed trainer on a pile of typewritten sheets and grabs it.

With inarticulate oaths Duffy gives chase along the pier. Instantly, the conga-line transforms itself into a rugby pack, the shoe being passed swiftly from hand to hand while Duffy ineffectually blunders from one tormentor to another. Finally, in his exasperation, he hurls the vodka flask he has been clutching at the ringleader, who has by now regained possession of Duffy's trainer. The boy makes a spirited attempt to fling it over the rail into the sea as the half-bottle shatters at his feet.

The commotion attracts the attention of a uniformed attendant who, with a cry of: 'Oy! Can't you lot read? No games!' disperses the flock of grounded starlings back towards the shore.

As Duffy hobbles to retrieve his trainer, which teeters perilously on the very edge of the pier, the attendant observes scornfully: 'As for you! You should know better at your age!'

Shoelace trailing, he shambles back to his bench where, to his mild surprise, he finds Gregory Coates deeply engrossed in the manuscript of *Palace Pier*.

Looking up, Coates says in a crisp, expert kind of voice, as if Duffy has been anxiously awaiting his opinion: 'This is good.'

'It's crap,' says Duffy, slumping down. 'Grade A, four-star crap, but crap.'

'No, I'm telling you, Mr Duffy. And I've only read fifty pages.'

'It gets worse.'

With an indulgent shake of the head, the agent says: 'That's what you all say. Christine Parrish. *Bringing Up Daddy*. She wanted to throw it in the Aga.'

'And did she?'

'Best-seller list for fourteen weeks. Now I don't profess to know everything,' says Gregory Coates knowingly. 'But this I do know. What you have got here is a best-seller.'

'Bollocks.'

'The only qualification I would make is that you should think about updating it. Now I can see why you did it as a period piece . . .'

And again bollocks. Someone else who couldn't write fuck in the dust on a venetian blind.

But Gregory Coates's voice trails off as both of them become aware of a heavily-made-up middle-aged woman in a mock-leopardskin coat hovering near the bench. She has caught his eye.

'So there you are. I was beginning to think you'd walked out on me.'

Confused and embarrassed, Coates thrusts the manuscript into Duffy's hands. 'Rather I thought it was the other way round,' he explains with heavy gallantry. 'I was just chatting to my friend.'

'There was a queue for the toilets. So are we going to that club or not?'

Gregory Coates gets hurriedly to his feet. To Duffy he says lamely: 'I'm being shown the sights. We'll talk tomorrow.'

The woman takes his arm as he shambles off, his face crimson under the twinkling pier lights.

Duffy sits for a long time, nursing the manuscript in his arms, like a baby. The breeze is no longer a breeze by now but a full-scale gust of wind, swirling around the pier and blowing out to sea. If Gregory Coates had not come along, that's where Mister Hamilton's last novel would be by now.

And where it ought to be. Why would anyone suppose Mister Hamilton left it in that trunk?

Best-seller? Who the hell knows? Mister Hamilton, except for his plays, was never a best-seller and there's no reason why he should start now.

All right, so the book would be coming out in Duffy's name but who will he think he's fooling? There are Patrick Hamilton buffs, people who know his work backwards, there may even be a Patrick Hamilton Society. And even if they couldn't prove anything, they'd know. And they'd be dismayed.

And the smart-arse critics would write how Mister

Hamilton's talent was destroyed by drink. How they'd seen it coming. The man from Hangover Square.

He can't put the script back in that Pandora's box of a trunk. And Duffy still has enough of the writer left in him never to be able to destroy someone else's original work. But there's such a thing as euthanasia.

As the wind howls about his ears he positions the manuscript of *Palace Pier* flat on the palms of his hands. Like a swooping gull, a dipping gust at once seizes and carries off the top few pages.

Soon a hundred pages are dancing and dipping in the gale like wartime leaflets ejected from an enemy bomber.

As Duffy sits motionless with the diminishing manuscript on his flattened hands there is a loud cannon-like bang that sets the gulls screeching and swirling aimlessly back and forth, weaving and ducking to avoid the purple-printed pages now soaring like kites out to and over the sea. It is the signal for the start of the fireworks that mark the end of the night's Festival activities.

A clutch of pages, perhaps two or three dozen, has descended with the bobbing wind and adheres, as from an upturned litter bin, to the rails and decking of the pier, illuminated momentarily by the fusillade of rockets that opens the firework display.

The attendant, who has been kicking the shards of the broken vodka flask under a bench, now officiously approaches Duffy as the last chapter of *Palace Pier* is swirled up into the night.

'If you're responsible for this mess, I'm going to ask you to leave the pier. Now.'

With an escort of screaming gulls, a cloud of purple typescript bobbing about his head, and a pretty confetti of golden sparks lighting the windy skyline above the Downs, Duffy trudges away.

Coming off the pier, he senses that someone is staring at him from a nearby bank of clanking slot machines. Someone he vaguely recognises.

Yes, he's got the bugger. Comes from Blackpool. Used to be a deck-chair attendant, went in Yates's Wine Lodge a lot. Went round claiming that he'd more or less written *Razzle-Dazzle*, just because he'd given Duffy one or two stories. Same as Maureen claiming to have written *Palace Pier*. Well, now it's blown out to sea, let her just try her hand at writing it again, then.

What's his bloody name again? Alladyce. Eric Alladyce. Him. Must be down for the Festival. He's written one or two novels on his own account since Duffy last clapped eyes on him. Northern, gritty stuff, not that Duffy's ever read any of it.

He is staring across at Duffy from the pin-table machine he has been idly playing. He recognises him all right. Malevolence written all over him. What he has to do now is to think up something hurtful enough for Duffy to remember for the rest of his life.

He gets it. It's not all that original, but it will serve.

He comes across.

''Scuse me. Weren't you Chris Duffy?'

KEITH WATERHOUSE

Soho

No London neighbourhood more resembles the restless down-stream tide of the Thames than the ragged square mile of Soho. Into its currents one evening slips Alex Singer, a student from Leeds in pursuit of his errant girlfriend. Twenty-four hours, three deaths, one fire and one mugging later, seduced, traduced and befriended, Alex is on his way to the Soho Ball.

'Effortlessly brilliant . . . a comedy of London life which tastes as fresh as a new-baked croissant'
David Robson, *Sunday Telegraph*

'The work of a master'
Hugo Barnacle, *Sunday Times*

'Keith Waterhouse is one of the most prolific and versatile of British comic writers and *Soho* finds him at his most entertaining and mischievous'
William Hartson, *Daily Express*

'A delightful novel'
John Torode, *Punch*

'As well as being a fast-paced farce, a string of encounters and incidents that could keep a full pub of people entertained for several evenings on end, Waterhouse's 13th novel is an elegy to a vanishing world. Soho the place may not be quite what it was, but in *Soho* the novel, Waterhouse brings it vibrantly to life.'
Juliette Garside, *Glasgow Herald*

'A wonderful evocation of a part of London the author loves and he has succeeded superbly in capturing its sleazy yet alluring nature, not least through the idiosyncratic characters who roam its streets and prop up its bars.'
George Osgerby, *Tribune*

SCEPTRE